Solis

....

Marybeth Ace

Copyright © 2024 by Marybeth Ace

All rights reserved.

No portion of this book may be reproduced in any form without written permission from the publisher or author, except as permitted by U.S. copyright law.

Contents

1. 1 — 1
2. 2 — 9
3. 3 — 16
4. 4 — 25
5. 5 — 33
6. 6 — 38
7. 7 — 45
8. 8 — 50
9. 9 — 59
10. 10 — 64
11. 11 — 71
12. 12 — 82
13. 13 — 89
14. 14 — 96
15. 15 — 104

16. 16	111
17. 17	128
18. 18	138
19. 19	149
20. 20	159
21. 21	170
22. 22	180
23. 23	192
24. 24	199

1

.

The castle was in a major uproar as their beloved friend, Quinn Fletcher had just awoken from his coma about three (3) hours ago and was now accepting visitors.

Soleil wanted to go see his best friend but wanted to also bring a gift for the younger man and he knew just the right person to go ask for help, even though she jumped at the sound of his voice.

So here he was now watching the main contributor to his dreams bake and decorate her beautiful confections for his friend.

However, he soon found himself becoming quite bored sitting in solid silence and decided to ask the young woman some questions in hope of quenching his ever-growing curiosity to get to know her.

"Lia, what did you do before you became our best chef?"

Blushing at the nickname that he had insisted on giving her, she stuttered out, "I was an f-figure skater."

"Woah! That's so cool! Do you have any pictures?!"

"Ask Reece, he has a-almost, if not all s-saved."

"Okay, what's your favourite colour?"

"Purple, you?"

"Yellow, which I think is the opposite colour to purple on the colour wheel!"

Nodding, she smiled slightly at his excited behaviour, even though he could not see her face at all as her back was facing him while she was decorating the brownies. She had designed then as different flowers because she thought it would be cute.

"Soleil, w-what is your favourite dish?"

"Hmm, I would have to say pork belly buns/ steamed bao buns, how about you?"

"Those are yummy! I love braised pork belly in soy sauce!"

Before he could say something, she twirled around with the container of decorated brownies and smiled brightly, while showing them off to him.

He complimented her work and praised her talent, which caused her caramel skin to flush pink.

As she tried to hand them over to the Irishman, he crossed his arms and shook his head. This left Ophelia confused and she asked him why he did that.

He explained to her that he wanted Quinn to meet her officially and also that he liked her company.

After that explanation, Soleil asked the Hispanic woman if she would accompany him to meet his friend.

For a split second, she was going to say no, but then she saw an unknown emotion swirling within the depths of the grey orbs, so she agreed.

As uncomfortable as she was around people, especially men, the brunette was intrigued by the older man and why he seemed to want to always talk to her.

Tightening her already firm grip on the handles of the glass dish, she smiled slightly and nodded for him to lead the way.

The pair made their way to the front door, thanking one of the thralls for opening the door for them and continued on their way. Suddenly, the blonde man stopped abruptly and this caused Ophelia to look up at him questioningly.

"What's wrong?"

"I just realised that I never asked you if you would like to walk or drive one of the cars to the infirmary."

"Well, how long is the w-walk?"

Scratching the back of his neck, he hummed and replied, "Probably ten (10) minutes, but that also might because I am so tall. You're quite short and it is adorable."

Pouting, the brunette woman huffed and muttered a quiet, "Nu-uh."

Chuckling at her reaction to his words, he could not help but stare at her beautiful face and for what felt like a decade, he just admired her.

Her flawless caramel skin with a beauty mark off to the side of her cheek and her gorgeous chocolate eyes that shone brightly when cooking.

The juicy lip that was currently jutting out because of her pout had the Irishman's mind filling with all kinds of thoughts, not that he'd act or voice them out.

He knew that she was not comfortable around him and would most definitely not appreciate him doing something.

Even though he pushed the filthy thoughts aside, Soleil continued to let his gaze trail across her body and he could not help but wonder how she would look in his shirts.

Ophelia had curves in just the right places and extremely toned from her years of figure skating. She was his dream.

Before he could continue to check her out and do more wishful thinking, he felt a light poke to his chest.

Grey orbs snapped up to meet dark brown ones and there was a massive spark that seemed to happen, she never looked him in the eyes before.

As fast as his eyes had met hers, she looked away and felt her face heating up quickly. Thanking quietly for her darker skin tone, her blush was less prominent and made her anxiety settle a bit more.

"You okay, Lia?"

"Y-yup, I was trying t-to tell you that I a-am okay with walking to the h-hospital."

"Oh sorry, I was just thinking about some stuff, but let's go."

Nodding, she followed closely behind him and hid behind him to keep away from the prying eyes of the thralls who had not seen her before.

The Irishman noticed that their stares were making the tiny woman behind him very uncomfortable and so he glared at them till they stopped.

Something inside of him hated how their eyes held looks of interest, lust and other things that made his blood boil.

He knew deep down that she was not his Valkryie and he did not know if she ever would be, but even so, he wanted to protect her.

By the time he had gotten out of his thoughts, the pair had reached the glass sliding doors of the club's infirmary.

Turning to face his companion, he shot her a quick smile before stepping into the sterile building.

Instantly after stepping in, all the single female eyes were on him and they were all looks filled with lust.

Normally, he would have returned the longing looks with a playful wink but now he only had eyes for one (1) woman and she was clutching a glass dish filled with brownies.

Not meeting any of their gazes, he placed a light hand on Ophelia's elbow and walked with her to the front desk.

The Irishman thanked Odin, himself that the person behind the reception was none other than Doctor Luke.

"Hey guys, are you here to see Quinn?"

"Yup, can you take us to him?"

"No problem, follow me."

The trio (3) walked down the narrow white halls toward the elevator and waited for it to be called. As they waited, Luke explained to them, their friend's condition and that he had been moved to a private room, on the request of King Elias.

He admitted that the staff had not a clue when he was going to wake up because when they estimated he would, he did not.

They suspected that he was regressing in his mind to try to create some sort of catalyst to block out the trauma and painful memories before he awoke.

By the time he was done explaining, they had reached the floor for the private rooms and he had to lead them to the last door at the end of the hallway. It had a silver plaque that read 'Quinn Fletcher.'

Knocking on the door, a muffled "Come in," was heard from the other side of the door and with that, Luke pushed open the door.

"Quinn, my boy, Soleil and someone new is here to see you."

"Okay."

With that, he turned back to face the duo and smiled. He let them know that it was alright to go in but reminded them quietly not to ask anything about what caused him to land up in the hospital in the first (1st) place.

Nodding, Soleil walked in and his companion followed in suit. The sight that greeted them was both a happy and sad one.

Happy, because it was good to see his friend awake and doing well for the first (1st) time in a good while.

Sad, on the other hand, because he looked so fragile and pale. He was also still hooked up to a good amount of machines that made sure nothing was going wrong. Looking at the heart rate monitor, they saw that his heart was still weak.

"Hey, big guy. How are you feeling?"

"I'm doing okay, still hurts to move. Who is this?"

"This is Ophelia, remember? Reece's little sister and-"

The blonde man nearly blurted out 'and my Valkryie,' which he knew for a fact was not true and also that the young woman in question would have not appreciated that.

"Oh yes! Sorry, my memory sometimes is still a bit foggy."

"T-that's okay. Oh! I baked you some chocolate fudge brownies, on r-request of Soleil."

After the words left her stuttering lips, the smile the gentle giant had spread across his face had lit up the entire room.

It was a beautiful sight to see his friend smiling once again as he used to before everything happened.

"Can I have one now?"

"Of course!"

Carefully, Ophelia slowly picked up a decorated baked good and placed it on a napkin before handing it to the hospitalised man. She watched nervously as he took a large bite of the gooey confection.

"OH MY GOD! This is so delicious! Please tell me the rest of those are for me."

Giggling, the Hispanic woman nodded quickly and placed the glass tray on the bedside table, next to his jug of water. The pair watched as Quinn quickly scarfed down the treat as if he was a starving man.

In a way, he probably was, since he never properly ate for a long time due to being in a coma, even though they pumped his body with fluids.

It could not compare to the real deal of tasting delicious home-cooked food and baked goods.

"Thank you so much."

"O-of course!"

"I'm glad to see you're okay, dude. We all missed you."

"I missed you all too."

2

"Thank you so much."

"O-of course!"

"I'm glad to see you're okay, dude. We all missed you."

"I missed you all too."

It had been a couple (2) of days since Quinn had woken up from his coma and since then, Soleil had spent every spot of free time he had with him.

He was extremely worried for his friend still and wanted to keep reminding him that he was loved by everyone.

Today, however, the gentle giant had shooed the blonde out of the hospital room, telling him to go talk to his lady, Ophelia.

This prompted the Irishman to protest and say that she was not his girlfriend nor his valkyrie. In return, he got an eye roll and a creepy smirk from his friend.

"Go on, I'm fine, sunshine. Just cause I was in a coma for a few months does not mean I'm blind. I could see how you looked at her. You want her bad, but I'm sure I don't have to tell you that you're going to have to take it slow with her."

"Yeah, I know. I was thinking of talking to Reece first (1st), since you know that's his baby sister. Plus, now that I think about it, none of us really know anything about them besides Elias and Nova."

"That is so true and good idea to talk to Reese's Pieces."

The nickname that the taller man had given to their chef friend was comedy gold. Soleil often died laughing whenever he heard it, it was that great.

Giving his friend a quick hug, Soleil said his goodbyes and exited the club's infirmary. He pulled his cellphone out of his jeans pocket and texted Reese.

S: Hey dude, you got a minute? I want to talk to you about something.

R: Yup, I'm not doing anything!

S: Okay, meet me in my room. I'm on my way back from the hospital, so I'll be there in like eight (8) minutes.

R: No problem, the door unlocked?

S: Yeah, go right in.

R: Alright, see you then.

The blonde man got to the front doors of the castle in no time and thanked the two (2) thralls who pulled open the doors for him.

Making his way through the first floor, he pressed the call button for the elevator and got in once it arrived.

Selecting his floor, he rocked back on his heels while it carried him up. He started thinking about what he was going to ask the Hispanic man.

He knew for sure that he was going to ask him to show him the figure skating pictures that he had of Ophelia.

Reaching the open door of his bedroom, he walked right in to see 'Reece's Pieces' sprawled out in a star formation on his king-sized bed, snoring.

Soleil normally didn't mind when his friends did stuff like this, but what was getting on his nerves was that the Hispanic man still had his filthy shoes on.

Walking quietly like a ninja over to the sleeping male, he knelt directly beside where his head was and inhaled deeply.

"GET YOUR STINKY ASS MOTHERFUCKING SHOES OFF MY CLEAN SHEETS, YOU SOITH!!!"

('Soith' translates from Irish to 'Bitch' in English.)

The frequency that the Irishman had yelled at had sent Reece flying up and off of his bed onto the floor.

From there he scooted all the way back to the far corner of the room, next to the wardrobe.

"Cé mhéad uair a dúirt mé leat gan do bhróga fucking a chur ar mo leaba?" Soleil muttered in an annoyed tone.

('Cé mhéad uair a dúirt mé leat gan do bhróga fucking a chur ar mo leaba?' translates from Irish to 'How many times have I told you not to put your fucking shoes on my bed?' in English.)

"I did not understand a damn word that just left your mouth, dude."

"I don't care. STOP DIRTYING MY FUCKING SHEETS WITH YOUR SHOES!"

Throwing his hands up in the air, the brunette winced at the sheer volume his friend's voice was reaching and quickly took off his sneakers, placing them by the door.

Slowly getting up, he went over and hugged his friend, mumbling an apology.

He knew how much of a neat freak the younger man was and he tried his best not to set him off as nice as the blonde was, that switch could quickly flip if you made a mess.

His little sister was the same way.

Once the pair separated, Reece looked up and asked him what is it that he wanted to talk to him about.

The look of seriousness that fell upon the Irishman's face had him standing up straighter and bracing himself for some bad news.

"I wanted to ask you to show me any photographs of Lia from her figure skating days?"

"Oh sure, how come?"

"I was talking to her the other day while she was baking the brownies that she made for Quinn and ended up asking her about herself."

Reece's eyebrows reached his hairline, "She actually answered you?"

"Yeah, I was surprised too."

"Wow, she must be starting to warm up to you."

"No fucking way man."

Fishing into the back pocket of his Levi's, the brunette unlocked his smartphone and went into his gallery. Scrolling, he quickly found the folder he had made and labelled, 'Ophbear's Skating Days.'

"Ophbear?"

Shrugging, he explained that he had nicknamed her that when she was born and that was how it was from that day forward.

Handing over his phone to his friend, he watched closely as the grey orbs admired every single photograph carefully.

Soleil was trying his best not to let his jaw hit the floor while he was looking through the professional pictures that were taken by photographers or ones (1s) taken by her brother on the ice.

She looked like she was peace with the world and there was a glimmer of confidence that shined through while she was performing.

It made him wonder what had caused that talented figure skater to remove herself from something she clearly loved.

Looking up, he met the same brown orbs that he was gawking at in the pictures, except it was Reece's. The blonde never noticed that the two (2) siblings were basically carbon copies of each other even with the four (4) year difference between them.

Blinking rapidly, he cleared his mind of memories of Ophelia as he had more important matters to deal with right now.

Which included knowing the past of the Diaz twins and what caused both of them to start working at the club.

"Reece, we need to talk, take a seat."

"Ohkayyyy?"

The older man shot him a puzzled look as he did not know what caused the other one's emotions to shift.

Taking a seat next to the Hispanic male, he looked him dead in the eye as he spoke.

"How did you come to work at the club? I never asked and you've been here for about eight (8) years before I came along."

Reece blew out a deep breath and his thin fingers clenched tight fistfuls of his jeans.

"The year I joined the club was the year our parents abandoned us. It had barely been a few days after my eighteenth (18th) and Ophelia was only fourteen(14). Our mother and father had packed a couple (2) of suitcases each, saying that they were going on a work trip and that they would be back in a week. That was a sack of fucking shit."

"What the fuck? I'm so sorry, dude. Please continue if you want to."

"It's okay. The day they were supposed to return, both of us had baked a cake for them as we knew how hard their jobs were. But, they never came and when the sun started to set, I received a phone call from their lawyer, letting me know that I was officially my little sister's guardian from that day forth. None of my questions was given answers, they left us with a trust fund of seven point five million dollars ($7,500,000). Money that we did not even know we had. A note was mailed to me saying that the house was now in my name, all the bills were taken care of for the next couple (2) of years and Ophelia was to continue her figure skating career."

Soliel could feel his blood start to boil at the thought of a young Reece and even younger Ophelia being abandoned by their parents, with no explanation whatsoever. Along with the fact that all these responsibilities dumped on his lap.

Wrapping his pale muscular arms around his friend's thin shoulders, he silently offered his comfort and it was gladly accepted.

"What happened then?"

"I started looking for a job, I did not want to use the money they left for us as I had no idea where it came from. I was always really skilled in the kitchen as my father taught me everything he knew and it sparked my love for the culinary arts. I guess it trickled down to my baby sister as well. Nowhere wanted to hire me and just when I thought I was going to actually have to open the account, Elias put out an ad for a chef. So I applied and was tested, then hired a day later. I owe this club everything because it's been eight (8) years and I have yet to touch the millions the left for us."

"I wish I knew you back then, my folks would have taken you in with open arms and all that stress would not have fallen onto you. I'm glad you managed to grapple with it and win, you raised Lia well. But, I do have to ask, what happened to make her so jumpy and have her quit the thing she seemed to love the most?"

Reece's chocolate brown eyes dropped to his lap, he explained to his friend that as much as he would love to help him understand his sister, it was not his place nor his story to tell.

He continued on letting Soleil know if he wanted to know, he would have to get her to trust him.

Not only that but be comfortable around him and not have her fumble over her words or run away from him.

"Fuck, that's gonna be hard, but I'm determined."

"I know you are, dude."

3

"Fuck, that's gonna be hard, but I'm determined."

"I know you are, dude."

A couple (2) of days had passed since Soleil had spoken to Reece and found out about them being abandoned, making the older man become a parent to his little sister.

The moment that his friend had left his room, he started pondering what to do with the information that he had received. It had taken him a while to figure it out, but now he had.

The blonde man had found it strange that these seemingly loving parents just decided to up and leave their children.

He just had a looming feeling hanging over him that something strange had caused their departure. His decision was made now, he was going to talk to his King to ask for permission to go under and see if he could find something to give the Diaz siblings closure.

Heaving himself off of his bed, he made his way over to the joined bathroom and zoomed through his morning routine.

The Irishman had just finished wrapping the indigo coloured fluffy towel around his slim waist when a knock sounded from his bedroom door.

A confused expression spread across his pale face and tightened his hold on the makeshift knot that was holding the fabric from exposing himself.

Walking over to the wooden door, he unlocked it and grasped the door handle.

The person who had knocked let out a large gasp and when his grey eyes lowered, he let out a large squeak and hid halfway behind the door.

"L-Lia, what are you doing here?"

The caramel skin of Ophelia's face was painted a bright red as all the blood in her body seemed to migrate there to expose her blushing.

Lowering her eyes, in her habit, she quickly realised that was a bad idea as her eyes met the older man's covered crotch.

Brown eyes met pale ones, with both parties looking completely embarrassed at the situation and they felt like neither of them could move.

Remembering that he asked her a question, she opened her mouth to speak but it seemed like her voice had left her.

"I-I, um, I was coming to tell y-you that breakfast was r-ready and I had set aside a plate with all of your f-favourites so that w-when you came down, it would n-not have been eaten."

A look of surprise graced Soleil's features, but as quickly as that expression had arrived on his face, it left and was replaced by a fond smile.

Raising his free hand, he patted the midnight black curls that sat on top of the head of the occupant of his thoughts.

This little act of affection sent her cooling cheeks back up in flames and she returned the smile, all while trying to understand this mysterious feeling that was bubbling inside of her. The moment he removed his hand, she felt herself missing his warmth.

Before Ophelia could panic and run away because of the foreign feelings, his deep Irish lilt reached her ears.

It took a few seconds for her brain to register what he said, but soon she realised he had thanked her.

"Of course."

"I'll be down in about five (5) minutes, I just need to get dressed, okay?"

"R-right! I'll set up your spot for you."

"You're the sweetest, thank you again."

"O-Oh thank you and of course."

With that being said, the Hispanic woman hurried away from his door and to the elevator with her cheeks on fire.

Soleil chuckled at how cute and shy she looked as she tried to make it not look like she was fleeing.

After the Irishman finished eating and insisting to the club's busboy that he would wash his dishes, he made his way to his friend/ King's office. Knocking, immediately he heard the deep voice saying, "Come in."

Pushing open one (1) of the giant doors, he was greeted by the usual sight of Nova in her husband's lap, but Ivan as well Benjamin was there.

All eyes were on him and normally that would not make him feel uncomfortable, but they all had smirks on.

The small hairs on the back of his neck stood up as the blonde felt as if he had just waltzed right into a lion's den and offered himself to be sacrificed.

Gingerly inching further into the massive office, he left the door slightly ajar in case he needed to book it.

"Close the door."

"It's closed."

"No, it's not, I'm not blind."

Heaving a big sigh, he knew there was no way he was going to get away with leaving an escape portal.

Doing as he was told, the quiet click resounding throughout the room and then he motioned to sit in the empty chair that sat in front of his desk.

"Good, now that you're seated, we can begin."

"Begin what?"

"Well, we were about to send Ivan to come to get you, but then you came knocking."

"Elias, that does not answer shit."

"Okay, okay. Ivan, here came to us with a request to start a new business for The Odin's Riders MC. I agreed to it since a lot of the members and horor want to take part."

"I still do not understand what the fuck this has to do with me though?"

A huge grin spread across Ivan's and he slapped Soleil's back with a resounding smack that had the younger man wheezing. Glaring at the noirette (a person with black hair), he delivered a quick punch to his shoulder.

"OW! FUCK! What was that for?"

"That's for nearly killing me by crushing my vertebral column and sending it into my lungs. Is asal tú."

('Is asal tú,' translates from Irish to 'You are an ass,' in English.)

"What did you just say?"

"I said, you are an A-S-S. A donkey, if you want it in nicer terms."

Before Ivan could open his big mouth to reply with a sarcastic retort, Benjamin stood up from where he was sitting quietly on the couch and made his way over to the two (2) bickering men.

'SMACK! SMACK!'

Simultaneous yelps of pain erupted from pair and two (2) sets of eyes glared at the male Herre.

"WHY!?"

"Cause the both of you are acting like children and we are trying to have a serious discussion here about the plans that one of you created. So quit your damn whining and get on with the actual matter. I left my wife alone with my children to come to help you both out, I'm not here to babysit."

Mumbling a quiet 'sorry,' the Irishman averted his gaze from the looming shadow and zipped his lips shut.

He knew how the other blonde man got when he was away from Serah and the twins, fatherly anger was not something he wanted to deal with.

"Ivan, tell Goldielocks what you wanted to tell him."

"Starry eyes, what is that nickname?"

"You're the male version of Goldielocks."

"I-, okay."

Waving his pale hand, Soleil motioned for his friend to tell him what he wanted to and to also hurry it up.

Grinning wildly, the noirette perked up in his seat and explained that the business they were going to open was an adult film one.

As if someone had lit a fire under his ass, the Irishman shot up and looked at him like he was either insane or grew a second (2nd) head. Placing his hand on his hip, he stared down at the seated man.

"What the fuck does this have to do with me? If you think I am going to take part in the films, I will shoot out your kneecap."

"Oh my Odin! NO! Jeez, who knew that such malevolence and violence were hiding behind that ray of sunshine."

Rolling his eyes, he replied, "Then what is it."

Seeing that his friend was losing a grip on his patience, Ivan decided to just spit out and said, "I want you to come along with me to oversee production."

"For how long?"

"Five (5) months."

"No."

"WHAT! WHY?"

"Because I have much better things to do than spending my time watching people fuck in front of cameras."

Soleil watched as the older male got onto his knees in front of him and clasped his hands together as if he was praying to a holy deity.

From the number of times his grey orbs had been rolled into the back of his head, he swore soon enough they were going to be stuck.

Repeating his previous answer, he made a move to step away when he felt a hand wrap around his ankle and a wail followed behind it.

"Släpp mitt ben."

('Släpp mitt ben.' translates from Swedish to English as 'Let go of my leg' or 'Release my leg.')

Removing herself from where she was curled on her husband's lap, watching the madness unfold, Nova made her way around the desk to her two (2) friends.

She could tell that the blonde was very close to snapping the other one's neck.

Placing a dainty hand on his shoulder, she shook her head at Ivan and told him to get off the floor as well as release the Irishman's leg. He did as he was told and went to sit back down in his chair.

Turning her attention to the annoyed man, she stared at him with a knowing expression and he gave her a slight nod of his head.

The other three (3) who sat in the massive room, realised that she knew something that they did not.

"Just go for a couple (2) of weeks, how about that? Just to help that idiot out."

He blew out a large breath, all of them watched as the normally exuberant man seemed to cave in on himself and a crestfallen look appeared on his face.

Wrapping her short arms around his tone abdomen, Nova whispered for only him to hear, "Look into it, it's okay."

Soleil nodding and mumbled a, "Thank you."

Now that he had the answer to what he was going to request, he felt marginally better and was finally able to focus on the other task at hand. Sitting back down, the blonde discussed the specifics and details about Ivan's idea.

Once that was over, he was told that the pair were set to leave tomorrow to drive to the outskirts of Stockholm to sort out any paperwork that needed to still be settled.

Then renovations would start and Soleil was tasked with interviewing the persons from the club who wanted to join at the building near the site.

That was his role for the next couple (2) of weeks along with managing the finances till Serphaina came back from a run.

It sounded easy enough, so he accepted his duties and excused himself from the office.

He had to speak to Ophelia to let her know where he was going and why he was leaving too. He did not necessarily need to inform her, but he wanted to.

The last thing that the blonde man wanted to do was make her feel as if he had left without a trace, like her parents.

The first (1st) thing he needed to do, however, was make a quick trip down the club's infirmary to visit Quinn and let him know that he wasn't going to be at the castle for a while.

Strolling through the glass sliding doors and into the sterile building, he beelined for his best friend's room.

Pushing open the door, he was greeted by the sight of the friendly giant slowly sitting down and laying back in bed, doing this all by himself.

"LOOK AT YOUUU!"

"AHHHHHHH!"

Soleil watched as his friend threw his blanket up in the air with fright as he had not seen his friend standing in the doorway and his yell scared the crap out of him.

"DUDE! You don't do that to a recovering person!"

Smiling sheepishly, he replied, "Sorry man, I just got so excited to see that you're starting to move on your own again."

"Yeah yeah, doesn't mean you nearly give me a damn heart attack."

Waving his hand dismissively, he explained to his friend what had happened earlier in the day from Ophelia knocking on his door and him opening it in his towel to the idea Ivan had. His best friend's eye turned to the size of saucers.

"Wowie, but I'm gonna miss you."

"I'll miss you too."

4

"**W**owie, but I'm gonna miss you."

"I'll miss you too."

(A couple (2) of days ago.)

"Hey, Lia. I need to talk to you about something real quick."

Seeing the dead-serious expression that was on the blonde man's face, she nodded quickly and dusted her both her hands to get rid of any flour on them.

Taking a seat on one (1) of the kitchen stools that were placed around the large marbled island, she looked up at him.

"W-what's up?"

Sighing, he explained to her what had ended up going down in their King's office and the reason why she would not be seeing him for a couple (2) of weeks.

His could feel his heart shatter at the crestfallen look that had spread across her face.

Her gorgeous brown eyes were slowly becoming glassy with unshed tears, which had them both surprised.

Her plump lips as well had curved into a frown and it was taking all the self-control that he had within him not to kiss her senseless.

Internally Ophelia was not only sad about the Irishman leaving, but also confused about why she was reacting the way she did.

In her mind, his departure would bring her some level of peace as he normally would always be near her, but that was not the case, she was sad.

"It'll only be for a couple (2) of weeks, I promise."

"I-I know."

"There's something else that I need to tell you."

"What is it?"

Before Soleil could reply, a very ecstatic Ivan bounded into the room and was physically shaking with excitement.

He placed his palms onto the younger man's shoulders and pushed down to elevate his hopping.

"C'MON! WE GOTTA GET GOING! I AM SO EXCITED, WE'RE STARTING A PORN BUSINESS!!!"

The second the word's flew out of the noirette's lips, the blonde's face paled as he was planning to tell Ophelia by easing her into it.

Unfortunately for him, Odin did not seem to be on his side today as the idiot known as his friend had dropped the bomb on her.

He was afraid to turn around and face her to see how she had reacted. Before he could act, he heard her stool scrape against the tiled floors of the kitchen and watched in defeat as she left the room without a word.

Turning his attention to the still babbling idiot, his grey orbs steeled over in anger and he quickly got up from where he was seated.

Making his way over, he loomed over the shorter man and without saying anything, raised his arm, smacking him upside the head.

Immediately after, Soleil walked out of the kitchen and through the front door to his car. He got in and sped off.

(Present Time.)

The moment that Ophelia had heard the two (2) words, 'Porn Business,' her mind went blank and she felt a spark of anger flare up inside of her.

It took her by surprise and that was why she had gotten up wordlessly to leave the room.

Now, after a few days had passed, she felt extremely bad for just leaving the room without telling the blonde man goodbye.

Her mind was telling her not to be too upset about it and not really try to get too close to him.

However, her heart was conveying a totally different message, she felt as if the internal organ was cracking under the gloom that had been plaguing her.

Deciding that she did not want to deal with these emotions right now, as well as not sit around, she briskly walked to the kitchen.

There is where the brunette would spend the next few (5) hours baking several different Swedish confections for all the members of the club.

She baked some almond caramel cake (also known as Toscakaka), St. Lucia Saffron Buns (Lussekatter), Swedish Cheesecake (Ostkaka) and miniature Summer Berries Pie.

No one dared to try to stop her or even so much as say a word to her and left her alone to her own devices.

Three (3) hours away Soleil was not having a good couple (2) of days. The entire time he had been away from the club so far, every little thing was pissing him off beyond his life's belief.

Not to mention, Ivan kept trying to speak to him and he kept ignoring.

Today was the day that he was to start interviews with the members, thralls and horror who wanted to take part in the business.

Even though all of them belonged to The Odin's Riders club, Elias made it known that it was going to be treated like any other outside business.

Meaning, just because you were affiliated or part of the club did not mean that you were going to be given a free pass into the jobs available.

Currently, the Irishman was sitting in one (1) of the many conference rooms that the hotel he was and the other members who were working on the site were staying at.

This was the room where he would be conducting all the interviews for the next few days.

Taking a glance at his Rolex that was sitting on his left wrist, he realised that Arin was about seven (7) minutes late and he could feel his anger spike.

Just as he was about to whip out his phone to call the man, he waltzed through the open door.

"Du är sen."

('Du är sen.' translated from Swedish to English is 'You are late.')

"Jag är ledsen, jag tappade tid."

('Jag är ledsen, jag tappade tid,' translated from Swedish to English is 'I'm sorry, I lost track of time.)

Rolling his grey orbs, he waved him over to where he needed to be seated and muttered a quiet, "Arís."

('Arís.' translated from Irish to English is 'Again.')

The minute that Arin's ass touched his seat, Soleil started the interview as he was on a tight schedule of having four (4) interviews today, including his and as well he had to go sort out the finances.

He was sent a document that contained all the questions he were supposed to ask.

The inquiries were:

1. What position are you applying for?

2. Why do you want this job?

3. If I were your supervisor and asked you to do something that you disagreed with, what would you do?

4. How do you feel about taking no for an answer?

5. Are you okay with being filmed during sexual acts?

7. Are you okay with having more than one sexual partner at a time?

8. Why should we hire you?

Once all the questions were asked and answered, the Irishman was wonderfully surprised at how professional his friend was when it was needed.

Another thing that had shocked him was extremely eloquent with his replies.

The blonde man decided he would be a good employee for Ivan's business and told him that he was hired.

However, he also told him that he needed to learn to be on time or even arrive at the building before he was supposed to.

Arin promised he would work on it and not him down, soon after the older man left. The rest of the interviews flew by quickly with all three (3) ending in success as he knew they would.

Considering the other applicants were Zara, Theo and Josh, who were all already very good at their jobs back at the castle.

Checking his watch again, he noticed that it was now quarter past two (2:15 PM) in the afternoon and he had yet to eat lunch.

Normally he would have just gone downstairs and eaten whatever delicious meal Ophelia whipped up, but he was not home.

Now that he was no longer occupied by other people, Soleil was hit with a wave of sadness and he quickly realised the source of his sadness. That was because he missed the beautiful, nervous, Hispanic ex-figure skater.

Before he could start to slip down the rabbit hole of depression, Astrid burst through the door with several bags of what looked like food. Making her way over to him, she plopped the parcels on his table.

"W-what is this? ALSO, WHEN DID YOU GET HERE?"

"Just now. It's some desserts and food made by Reece. Well, the food is, the sweet stuff was made by the little snow fairy."

"Who?"

"Ophelia, you idiot."

The Asian woman watched as her friend's mouth formed into an 'O' shape and his cheeks flushed a bright pink.

It was quite noticeable since he was so pale and she felt the need to tease him about his little crush.

Back at The Odin's Riders castle a brother and sister were sitting down in the garden at the back of the building to have a serious talk.

Reece had received a text from his little sister to meet him there because she had something she wanted to ask him.

When he had turned the corner, he immediately knew something was wrong with his sibling because her eyes were filled with unshed tears.

Rushing over to her, he immediately went about giving her a once over to make sure she was physically ok.

"What's wrong, my little bear?"

She opened her mouth to tell him the reason why she was about to cry, when her brain told her not to.

She had no idea how her big brother would react to her saying that she missed his friend and quickly decided not to.

"I-I just miss mom and dad."

Hearing the words that left her lips, Reece immediately wrapped his arms around her and started to rub her back.

He knew that she was deeply affected by their departure from their lives but he also knew she was hiding something, though he did not know what.

Whatever it was, he would not push her and would wait for her to come to talk to him about it like she always had.

"I know you do, me too."

Soleil was back in his hotel room laying on his bed, staring at the ceiling and thinking over what he had just done.

He had sent his Herre, Zia all the information that he could find about the Diaz siblings parents and asked the Russian woman to see what she could find.

She promised that she would move quickly and hopefully have something to give him within the next four (4) days or less.

Sighing, the blonde hoped that there would be something that was found to give them some answers.

"I really fucking hope we find something. Ophelia and Reece, please forgive me for digging."

5

"I really fucking hope we find something. Ophelia and Reece, please forgive me for digging."

It had been exactly four (4) days before he had received anything from Zia. Every time he had messaged or called her about any progress, it was met a frustrated "No," as everything seemed locked by something or someone.

The Russian informed him that he was definitely correct on his hunch that something odd had happened because a lot of information that would normally be public was locked or gone.

She told him whoever or whatever caused them to disappear did not want anything to be found.

Fortunately for the pair, the Riders had an excellent tech team and they had worked on finding out everything that their Herre could not.

Before they had a chance to panic, Aster, their main hacker contacted Soleil and let him know they found everything.

Currently, he was going over all the documents and prints that they had Astrid bring over from the club.

There were so many things that did not make sense to him and it seemed like all of it was gonna come up to be a dead end.

As he threw down the last file, his grey eyes caught sight of something. Many of the files had similar names on them with all of them belonging to the same company. This was not one that he had recognized and he had no idea where to start.

One (1) thing he was certain about was that whoever and whatever this business was, they definitely had something to with the older Diaz's disappearance.

The day they left was the last time anyone had seen them.

It was as if they had vanished without a trace and no one seemed to know anything about it. He also found it weird that no one had filed a missing person's report besides Reece.

Even there was not a single police report besides his on it and nothing about an investigation.

Deciding that he needed to ask someone else for help, a person who had the resources to dig up the truth as well as someone he trusted.

He knew the right person he was going to recruit for it and that was his older sister's fiance, Cillian McCarthy, who was a private investigator.

Grabbing his phone, he dialled his number and waited anxiously for him to pick up. Shortly after he heard the heavy Irish lilt of his soon to be brother in law.

"Hey, Solar System. What brings on the unexpected call?"

"Stop it with that stupid nickname, I really wish that Dinah did not tell you about that. Anyways, Cilly, I was calling to ask you if you would be able to look into something for me?"

"Of course, what is it?"

The younger man went on to explain everything in detail and also went through the files with him on the phone.

"What's the name of the company?"

"Its called 'Evergreen Engineers,' I've never heard of them before."

"Hmmm, it might not be from Sweden that's why. Didn't you say that the parents and the son were born in Spain, but the daughter was born in Sweden?"

"Yep, there is no information on why they left. It just seems like they upped and left without much notice beforehand."

"Hmmm, that's very strange. I'll start from there. I'll fly to you in about a week since I remember you mentioning to Dinah that you were not at the castle for a couple (2) weeks."

"Alright and yeah, by the time you come I should be back at the club."

"Okay, well I'll talk to you later, my fiance is calling me."

"Shut up, stop reminding me that I am very much single. Bye."

Soleil heard loud laughter emitting from the receiver as he removed the phone from his and he hung up.

He blew out a deep breath of relief as he had been expecting his brother in law to be a little apprehensive about helping since his wedding was a little over a month away.

However, he was pleasantly surprised at how quick Cillian had agreed and even more so that he had suggested flying out to him.

Getting up from his bed, the Irishman gathered all the scattered notes and documents into their designated piles.

Once he had gotten them sorted out, he packed them back into their envelopes and placed them in the hidden safe in the wall.

The last thing he wanted was for those papers to be found and stolen because that could cause trouble for the siblings.

Taking a seat by the window in his room, his eyes scanned the view in front of him of the pool and hot tub of the hotel.

He saw a lot of his friends either relaxing by the water on the lounge chairs or were swimming.

The blonde decided that he would join them since they all had finished all that they had been tasked with for that day and they deserved a little break.

Just as he was about to head out of his room, his phone pinged with an incoming text.

It was from his sister, Dinah's text read, "Hey baby brother! Just wanted to let you know we chose the theme for the wedding, WINTER WONDERLAND! We're even going to have ice skating at the reception so you better learn quickly before you fall on your ass! Love you!"

Groaning loudly, Soleil ran his hand through his golden hair and tugged at it. His sister knew how bad his balance was on the ice and he knew for a fact that she would want some intricate dancing in the rink.

Looking up to the ceiling, he stared at the chandelier and muttered, "Why me?"

An hour (1) later his phone had once again made a text notification sound which drew his attention from where he was in the pool splashing Astrid.

Pulling himself out of the warm water, he saw that it was a text from Reece.

"Ophelia's been acting weird today so I sent her to speak to Lyra and Serah. I don't know what's going on inside her head and I'm worried."

"Keep me updated please, she's strong and will be okay."

"Thanks, man."

"Of course."

6

✷ This chapter takes place the same day as the previous.*

"Ophelia's been acting weird today so I sent her to speak to Lyra and Serah. I don't know what's going on inside her head and I'm worried."

"Keep me updated please, she's strong and will be okay."

"Thanks, man."

"Of course."

Ophelia had been mindlessly wandering around the castle for the whole day as she was basically thrown out of the kitchen by Benjamin as he found that she was working too much.

So since then, she had no idea what to do because the one (1) thing she was using to distract herself was gone.

Ever since the tall blonde Irishman had left to go work on the project that Ivan had started, her heart had felt heavy and she was constantly depressed.

It was not like her to act like this and she had no clue on why she was.

Any time she thought about what the purpose of the new business was or someone brought it up, her thoughts were plagued with images of him engaging in the filming aspect. This sent a red hot fire through her veins and it shocked her.

It had been exactly six (6) days and everyone in the castle had started to catch on to her down mood.

Normally she was quite upbeat and happy despite being scared of half (1/2) of the club, but now they were all wondering what happened.

The one (1) person who was worried more than anyone was, of course, Reece.

He was genuinely baffled by her recent behaviour and even though he had picked up on something being wrong a couple (2) of days ago, he still had no context.

His little sister was still trying to dart around going to talk to him and it made him upset because he wanted to know if there was anything he could do to make it better. The younger Diaz sibling was aware of how her brother was feeling and that added to her gloom.

Finally, Ophelia mustered up the bravery and courage she normally lacked to go ask him for some advice on why she was feeling this way. She had no clue how he would react nor if he would have any answers to give her.

Making her way through the long castle hallways, she arrived at the bedroom door she was looking for and knocked. From inside the room, she could hear a pair (2) of muffled voices and rustling of sheets.

Her eyes widened when her brother opened up his door without his shirt on and was only wearing his navy blue sweatpants.

Peeking underneath his raised arm, she was met by the sight of one of the waiters laying in his bed.

If she remembered correctly his name was Reid, though that was not really important to her now as she brought her gaze back up to her, now blushing brother's face. The tips of his ears were bright red and she could practically see the heat radiating off of them.

Raising a perfectly arched eyebrow, she watched as he smiled meekly at her and nervously rubbed the back of his neck.

Shaking her head, she raised a small hand and waved at the older man, who smiled gently in return.

"Podrías haberme dicho, no me habría enojado, sabes."

(Translated from Spanish to English, "You could have told me, I wouldn't have gotten mad, you know.")

"Sí lo siento. Yo debería."

(Translated from Spanish to English, "Yes, I'm sorry. I should.")

Nodding she smiled and told him she was happy for both of them. As she turned to leave, his hand grasped her wrist and asked her what had she come by for. The wooden floor was suddenly very interesting to her as well as her feet.

Poking her, Reece kept asking her what was it and he knew she would give in soon because he as tickling her sides slightly. He could tell that she was fighting back a small smile and a giggle.

"Fine, fine! I wanted to ask you if you ever felt yourself getting angry over something or someone that was not yours?"

"No, sorry. I think you should talk to Lyra or Serah! OO! Or both of them."

"You think so?"

"Yeah, since Nova's mom had arrived, she's been flocked by everyone for any advice, I guess because of everything she had been through. Same with the little strawberry."

"Okay, I'll go find them."

"I think they're at her salon right now, from what I heard from Benjamin at least."

"Alright, I'm happy for you, I wish you two (2) the best."

"Thank you."

Smiling, she waved goodbye and turned on her heel, walking down the hallway from the direction she came to return to the elevators.

As she waited for the moving metal contraption to take her to the first (1st) floor, her mind wandered to how would she explain it to the two (2) women.

Still lost in thought, she barely heard the loud ding of the elevator as the silver doors slid open and one (1) of the thralls calling her name.

The moment she felt a hand touch her shoulder, her brown orbs snapped up to an unfamiliar face.

An uncontrollable sense of fear coursed through her veins like a rushing river and a scream bubbled up but got caught in her throat. Just as she was about to let out a loud wail, Serah's voice rang out.

"OI! TAKE YOUR HAND OFF OF HER! DON'T YOU KNOW SHE'S TERRIFIED OF MEN!"

Ophelia watched with wide eyes as the strawberry blonde grabbed the young guy's lower arm and flipped him.

She barely caught when the older woman said, "Learn to listen." Making her way over the speechless chef, she graced her with a gentle smile.

"Hey, gorgeous. You ok?"

"Uhhh, yes, thank you! I was actually looking for you and also...Lyra."

"Oh? Both of us? Well, this works out perfectly because I was going to head by her now with the twins. My hubby was bringing them to me."

"Aww, they are the cutest little things ever! How old are they now?"

"About a year (1) and seven (7) months now. My babies are growing up so fast!"

The Hispanic woman giggled at the dramatic actions of her friend before she could utter a reply, Benjamin appeared with Jasper sitting on his shoulders, tugging at his hair. While his twin sister was sitting on his boot-clad foot and clutching tightly to her father's leg.

He looked like he was in desperate need of help and with a panicked expression in the direction towards his wife, she immediately switched to mother mode.

"Jasper Nilsson! Let go of your father's hair. Miss Harper Nilsson, come here."

Ophelia watched in awe as both of the children instantly stopped what they were doing and did exactly as they were told.

Serah gently picked up her daughter and with her in her arms, she turned to the younger woman.

"Would you mind holding Jasper?"

Smiling brightly, she replied, "I would love nothing more."

That was how Lyra found them at the front desk of her salon that sat near the club's infirmary and she nearly died from how cute the sight was.

Making her way over to the small quartet, she greeted them and ushered them to one of the private spa rooms.

Once they were all seated, the three (3) women made small chitchat and caught up with one another while the twins played on the floor.

While they were speaking about how Lyra's business was going, Ophelia felt a slight tug on her pants leg.

Looking down, she was met by a pair of familiar-looking blue eyes and a chubby little face who was grinning widely at her.

She watched as the toddler raised his arms above his head and made grabby motions in her direction.

"Ups! Ups!"

"Aww look at you, little cutie pie!"

Carefully picking him up, she let him play with the ends of her hair as she continued with the conversation.

After about fifteen (15) minutes had passed, the youngest woman piped up and asked the other two (2) if she could ask them something.

"Of course."

"Anything, honey."

Looking down into her lap, she averted her gaze from her new found friends and to the now sleeping little boy.

"I was wondering...if you guys had any advice for how I've been feeling lately."

Serah rested a dainty hand on her knee and asked her to explain exactly what she meant by that.

"Well, I'm sure you guys have noticed at the castle, I have not exactly been my usual self. Six (6) days ago it had started.... I keep feeling as if there is a storm cloud constantly looming over my head and it just doesn't want to dissipate."

"Hmm..well is there a particular event that happened right before the gloom happened?"

Ophelia made a small humming sound as she placed her chin in her hand and thought about the question.

It took her a few minutes, but the realisation struck her like a bolt of lightning as her head shot up, she tried to not jerk her body as to not wake Jasper.

"It was right after Soleil told me that he was leaving for a couple (2) of weeks."

A pair of smirks appeared on Serah and Lyra's face as they shared a knowing glance between one another.

She watched as they started to giggle and wiggle their eyebrows at her, which made the younger woman sink into the cushions.

"Sweetie..."

"Let us help you...."

"You like Soleil."

"You have a crush on the Irishman."

"WHAAA-"

7

"Sweetie..."

"Let us help you...."

"You like Soleil."

"You have a crush on the Irishman."

"WHAAA-"

For the past few days, all Soleil could think about was how he was going to ask Ophelia to teach him and how to get her to agree.

The last thing he wanted to do was make her feel pressured to help, but he also did not want to be taught by anyone else.

It had been dead end after dead end and it was driving him absolutely mad. Not to mention, Cillian still had barely any news for him on what had happened to the Diaz parents, it had proven to be a lot more difficult than they had foreseen.

Sighing, the blonde man slammed his head down onto the long wooden table in the conference room and groaned out loud, everything was falling stagnant. The sound of the door being pushed open had his head flying up and staring at Ivan.

"What do you want."

"Damn, that's cold! Are you seriously still angry with me? It's been over a week nowwww!"

He rolled his grey orbs into his head as he listened to his friend stomp his foot like a damn toddler, sometimes he could not believe that this man was twenty-seven (27) years old. Most of the time, it felt as if the older man was actually five (5).

Shaking his head, he ignored his guest and turned his attention back to his laptop screen as he was looking at tuxedos before he forgot to get one (1) for Dinah's wedding.

He had so many things he needed to get done that he had nearly brushed passed it.

A hand soon fell onto his sagged shoulder and he looked up to see the noirette staring at him with a concerned expression.

Ivan dragged a chair from the side of the table and placed it next to his friend, taking a seat almost immediately.

"What's wrong? There have been very few times I have seen you so upset."

"Dinah informed me that they planned to have ice skating at the reception and you know damn well I do not know a single fuck about that. So, I had been thinking about asking Lia, however, I'm not sure she'll even agree nor do I know how to ask her."

"Dude, just ask her. Even though she's terrified of the rest of us, besides Elias, Benjamin and of course Reece, a blind man could tell that she isn't as scared of you. I hate to admit it but you're the only person she seems to relax, albeit only slightly when you're near her. So, ask her and she's more than likely going to agree."

Soleil gave his friend a gentle smile and quietly thanked him. It warmed his heart to know that she was somewhat fonder of his presence than he had initially thought. Immediately, the gears and cogs in his mind started moving to formulate a plan.

He spent the rest of the day focusing on sorting out the finances for Seraphina because his two (2) weeks of working there were almost up.

The main reason for dedicating all of his time to the paperwork was because he wanted to have all his focus on Ophelia and their parents.

Putting down his pen onto the closed file, the Irishman ran his hand through his blonde locks and cracked his neck before letting out a tired groan.

Opening his eyes, he looked at the clock and his grey eyes widened as he saw the clock read a quarter to eleven at night (10:45 PM).

Rubbing his hands over his face, he tried to rub as much of the sleep out of his eyes and started to gather his things to put them in his briefcase.

Once he was done packing up, he made his way out of the room and up to his bedroom.

Resting his case in another one of the secret safe's that was hidden within the room, the young man removed his tie and unbuttoned his shirt.

Throwing them into his hamper, he quickly stripped out of the rest of his clothing and rested his phone on the bathroom counter.

Soleil turned on the taps for the tub and adjusted them to get the right temperature for the water.

As he waited for the bath to heat up, he shuffled through the hotel's complimentary bath products before deciding he'd use a rose bath milk because he liked the smell.

Cutting off the water flow, he poured in the bottle as it was a single-use and mixed it into the water with his hand. The blonde man took a moment to just allow the rose scent to brush over his senses and relax him.

Sliding into the warm water, he released a loud content sigh and leaned his head against the back of the tub.

Closing his eyes, he just floated in the milk bath and let his mind wander. His first (1st) thought was always Ophelia and how much he missed her presence.

Slowly it drifted from that to the plan that he had concocted to ask her because he wanted to show her that he wanted her and only her to teach him.

Phase one (1) of the plan started tomorrow morning, where he would send her a bouquet of her favourite flowers which were lily of the valley.

The next day, the Irishman would send her a trilogy of cookbooks that she had been raving about wanting to get for weeks.

He may or may not have asked Astrid and Nova to let him know what as something she really wanted.

On the final day before he'd be returning to the club, he decided to get her a custom made apron and chef's hat with her name. Along with that, the smock would have a cute commissioned design of a teddy bear because of Reece's nickname.

Then when he got back to The Odin's Riders castle, he would sit her down over some food and ask her about his situation.

He hoped that all of this would be enough for her to realise that he not only wanted her to help him but that he cared about her as well.

However, there was another worry on his mind. He was scared that it would come across too strong and reveal his true feelings for her which would actually make her more terrified of him that before.

"Fuck this is complicated. I'll go through with it and I fucking hope it works out the way I want it to, or else I'm gonna dig my grave."

8

"Fuck this is complicated. I'll go through with it and I fucking hope it works out the way I want it to, or else I'm gonna dig my grave."

Three (3) days before Soleil's return.

"HEY OPHELIA! THERE'S A DELIVERY FOR YOU!"

The loud scream that came from the front foyer of the castle made the young woman nearly drop the hot pot of soup that she was carrying. Huffing out angrily, she rolled her eyes and stomped out of the kitchen.

"Benjamin Nilsson. You do not yell at a chef when they are in their domain. I could have dropped steaming hot soup all over the floor but even more so ME!"

Her friend's blue eyes widened in shock and he started to repeatedly apologise as that was the last thing he wanted to cause.

On the inside though, the Herre of the club felt his whole body warm at the fact that she really wasn't scared of him anymore and she had only been here for almost a year (1).

The Hispanic woman made her way around the taller man and over to the front door where there was a florist delivery woman was standing. She smiled at her and asked her to sign on the dotted line.

Once she had done that, she was handed a medium-sized box and wished a good day. Carrying the package into the kitchen, she gently placed it onto the marbled counter. Grabbing a pair of scissors, she cut the tape and peered in.

Letting out a loud squeal, she started to jump up and down in excitement. Nova and Elias came running in along with Benjamin to see if everything was okay.

The trio (3) visibly sagged in relief when they realised she was just happy.

"Hey, chef! What did you get?"

"I got a vase of my favourite flowers! Look!"

Carefully, she removed the expensive ornate looking glass container that housed a large set of said flora.

The spicy, sweet and lemony scent of the flower permeated the kitchen which brought Ophelia such fond memories of her figure skating days.

She remembered that whenever there was a tournament her fans, brother and friends would send her these specific flowers if she won or even if she did not. It was her comfort item for a long time but then for a few years, it was not anymore.

Before her train of thought could go down a deep dark rabbit hole, she was interrupted by Nova saying, "Look, there's a card!"

Turning her attention to where her friend was pointing, she noticed a pastel yellow cardstock and she picked it up.

Flipping it over, her brown eyes widened as she read the message.

The note read, "For my culinary genius! From your favourite Irishman, Soleil."

That day, Ophelia could not stop smiling for the life of her and could not stop throwing glances at the flowers.

Two (2) days before Soleil's return.

As per usual, the young chef was in the kitchen whipping up some delicious concoctions when she was once again called because she had another delivery. This confused her because she did not remember ordering anything.

In her mind, she did not think for a second that it was from the blonde man. In the hallway, Zia was standing there holding a large box and this sight caused Ophelia to rush forward. She started fretting over having the older woman hold this heavy box for so long.

The Russian woman just smiled at her and shook her, letting her know that she did not mind nor was it a bother to her whatsoever. The younger woman sighed and ushered for her to set it on the counter.

Doing the same thing she did yesterday, she gasped and lifted up the cardboard bookcase that held all three (3) of the recipe books by her favourite chef.

Immediately her eyes were drawn to a pastel purple card stuck to the top of the first (1st) book.

It read, "I heard you really wanted these, but could not find them. I hope you love them and cook amazing dishes from these books! From your favourite idiot, Soleil."

This warmed her from head to toe and these wonderful gestures were making her fall deeper into her feelings for the older man.

One (1) day before Soleil's return.

It was around seven o'clock in the morning (7:00 AM) when Ophelia heard a knock on her bedroom door and when she answered it, there was no one there. However, there was a yellow and purple floral gift bag sitting right in front of her door.

Warily, she grabbed the ribbon handles and brought into her room, where she placed it on top of her vanity. Reading the card, it just read, "From Soleil :)" and that alone was enough to make her smile.

Taking out the kite paper, she saw two plastic packages and she decided to reach in for the smaller one (1) first.

Unwrapping it, she saw that it was an offwhite chef's hat with a teddy bear that was the same shade of brown like her eyes.

She did the same for the other item and giggled at the design on the front of the apron.

It was the same bear that was on her hat but also a larger cream coloured bear that was seated next to the other. Under the pair, it read, "Lia."

She wore it all day while she was in the kitchen and tried her best not to get it dirty.

The day Soleil comes home.

The Irishman woke up bright and early with a massive smile on his face as he was finally leaving this damn hotel to head back home.

Seraphina had arrived yesterday afternoon and he spent the rest of the day showing her around along with where everything was.

Now it was time for the young man to jump into his car and make his way back to the heart of Stockholm.

Picking up his bags, he packed them into the trunk of his car and sat behind the wheel, waving at his friends before he sped off.

On the drive back home, Soleil noticed that there was a very obvious black SUV trailing his carmine red Bugatti Divo.

Narrowing his eyes as he looked in the rearview mirror, he could make it out there were four (4) persons in the vehicle.

Checking again, he could tell that they were all men from the size of their builds which made him smile.

The last thing he wanted to do was hurt a woman unless he really had to, his mother taught him better than that.

Speeding up, the blonde wove through the traffic carefully and on the Bluetooth of his car, he made a call to his King.

"Elias, someone's tailing me."

"How many cars?"

"One (1) SUV, but there are four (4) men inside from what I can tell."

"Okay, Zia has tracked your location and a team is on their way. Go to the shopping mall and get inside. Go into SUITSUPPLY and wait there, but stay hidden."

"Alright."

"You have any weapons on you?"

"I have my knives and two (2) CZ 75B strapped under my jacket."

"Use it only if needed."

"Got it, bye."

"Bye."

Hanging up, the Irishman checked his mirror again and noticed that the car that was trailing him was quite far behind.

Not one (1) to get cocky, he drove a little faster than the rest of the vehicles, making sure not to make it obvious that it's him.

Seeing the mall within sight, he followed the car in front of him to the entrance of the parking lot, he chose not to park underground as that would have him trapped.

Parking near a lot of red cars, Soleil quickly got out and started walking at a leisurely pace to not seem suspicious.

As he walked through the glass sliding doors, he saw the black SUV driving into the underground parking lot.

This action made him smile widely, the young man would inform his friend once he got to the spot that he was ordered to go to.

Ducking into the store, the blonde sent a quick text and then he started to pretend to browse the shirts in the back when he felt a light tap on his shoulder.

Grey orbs widened in surprise when he saw that the person who had touched him was none other than Alexander Clarke.

The tall muscular man was one (1) of the very few nomad members of The Odin's Riders MC and he was rarely seen in Stockholm.

To say he was shocked was an understatement, his surprised look was met by a mere cheeky wink.

"W-what are you doing here?"

"I was passing through when bossman called and told me you needed help."

"Oh well, thank you."

"Not a problem, however, the minute the problem is resolved, I am out of here."

Nodding in understatement, the pair scanned the large store for anyone out of place and found nothing. They stayed within the store for about fifteen (15) minutes before they saw three (3) very familiar faces.

Astrid, Benjamin and Lennox strolled right on in, staring right at them with massive stupid grins spread across their features.

Rolling his eyes, Soleil made his way over to them and were told that they apprehended the four (4) men who were following him.

"Who's watching them right now??"

"No one, they're unconscious and chained up. They tried stabbing Astrid."

"Oh."

"Anyways, let's go home."

Waving goodbye to Alexander, the Irishman hopped back into his car and with his friends following him, they all went back to the castle. Parking in his designated spot, he popped the trunk open and grabbed his belongings.

The second he walked through the front door, he was thrown backwards onto the wooden floor and an excited Reece was sitting on top of his chest.

Placing his hands on his friend's shoulders, he tried to push him off but the older man was heavier than he looked.

"Reese's Pieces, can't breathe."

Getting off his friend, he lightly slapped him on his shoulder and rolled his eyes.

"Are you calling me fat?"

"No, now shut the fuck up. Why did you try to make me one (1) with the floor?"

The Hispanic man just smiled cheekily and shrugged, then extended his hand out to help him up. Allowing himself to be pulled up, he hugged his friend and let him know that he had indeed missed him.

A loud gasp made the pair separate and standing there in the doorway of the kitchen was none other than Ophelia in her apron that he had bought for her.

Forgetting about her crippling shyness for a moment, she ran up to him and jumped into his arms.

This action shocked Soleil but at the same time made his cheeks and tips of his ears flush a bright pink.

Sooner than he would have liked, the younger woman made a move to get down and he reluctantly let her.

Once their eyes met, her caramel skin was a deep red because she had just realised what she had done. She had just missed him so much and she had no idea what had come over her.

Clearing her throat, she smiled shyly at him and murmured a quiet, "Welcome back home."

She peeped up through her lashes and saw that he too was looking quite a bit flustered. This made her glad to know he was affected by her.

"Um, I made y-you some pork bao b-buns because I know you told me they were your favourite."

"Thank you! Uh, I hope you liked the gifts."

"Oh! I loved them s-so much, thank y-you!"

Smiling, he followed behind her into the kitchen and listened to when she pointed to the cushioned stool on next to the island.

Soleil watched with a fond look in his eyes as she dishes out about four (4) of the Asian dish for him.

"Here you go!"

"These look absolutely incredible! Please get some for yourself and join me, Lia?"

"T-thank you and alright."

Ophelia quickly prepared a couple (2) for her and took the seat right next to the object of her newfound affections.

They ate in comfortable silence and once they had both finished eating, the pair washed the dishes together.

"Lia, I need to ask you for a favour."

"O-okay."

"My older sister's wedding is coming up and she is having a skating rink rented for her reception, but the problem is that I can't balance on the ice for shit. So, I was wondering if you would help teach me because you're amazing with the skates. I don't want anyone else to teach me, so please, will you help me out?"

"Of course."

9

"Lia, I need to ask you for a favour."

"O-okay."

"My older sister's wedding is coming up and she is having a skating rink rented for her reception, but the problem is that I can't balance on the ice for shit. So, I was wondering if you would help teach me because you're amazing with the skates. I don't want anyone else to teach me, so please, will you help me out?"

"Of course."

A day after 8

Soleil was woken up by his phone ringing, which annoyed him greatly, especially when he saw the time that his brother-in-law was calling him.

Picking up the call, he growled out a low, "What do you want and five in the morning (5:00 AM)?"

"Well, aren't you a ray of sunshine?"

"What. The. Fuck. Do. You. Want."

"Okay okay, I'm calling to let you know that I found a lead on the thing that you asked me to look into. I'm on a flight to the destination now, so I won't need to fly over to you, okay?"

"That's good and fine. Now goodnight."

"Goodni-"

The blonde hung up the phone before the older man could finish speaking and he rolled back over on his bed, quickly falling back asleep.

The next time he is woken by a knock on his door, quickly checking the time, he saw that he had overslept.

Calling out to the person who was still tapping on his bedroom door to come in, he watched with tired eyes as Zia popped her head in.

Seeing that he was still wrapped up in his blankets, she let out a small laugh and quickly informed him that Astrid wished to speak with him.

Nodding, he waved at her and once she left, the Irishman fell back onto his pillow. Desperately trying to rub the sleep out of his eyes and stretched, releasing several loud groans when he fell his bones pop.

Slowly getting out of bed, he did his regular morning routine and then made his way over to his wardrobe.

He grabbed his dark purple t-shirt, a pair of black ripped jeans, his infamous leather jacket and threw on his combat boots.

He strapped his knives into place and also placed his guns into their holsters. Spraying on some cologne, he stuck back in his five (5) earrings and fixed his hair. Deeming himself ready, he grabbed his things and left.

"Good morning, Leprechaun."

Rolling his eyes, he looked down at the tiny Asian woman that was also known as Astrid Blix and stuck his tongue out at her. Laughing, she waved for him to follow her to the dining room and told him to take a seat.

"Zia told me that you needed to speak to me."

"Yes, I do. The four (4) men that were tailing you yesterday are dead, but that really does not matter. Anyways, they admitted to why they were following you after a little convincing from me."

"Why?"

"They wanted to see if they could kidnap you and hold you for ransom."

"From the club?"

"Yes, they were a quartet of kidnappers that have been on the run for about eight (8) years now, well were on the run."

Chuckling, he shook his head at the trigger happy smile that was plastered across his friend's face.

He knew how much she enjoyed what she liked to call 'convincing' their enemies or anyone who tried to bring harm to the club.

Later in the day, around one-thirty in the afternoon (1:30 PM), Ophelia and Soleil had just arrived at the skating rink that Elias had rented out for the next few weeks for them.

They were allowed to be in there privately from two o'clock to five o'clock (2:00 PM - 5:00 PM).

They had gotten there a little bit earlier as the seasoned figure skater wanted her student to put on the skates and practice walking in them before heading out on the ice. The pair had just put them on and she started by demonstrating how to move.

After repeating it a few more times, she had him stand up and try. Surprisingly, he got the hang of it pretty quickly and this made the blonde happy.

He continued to practice just simple walking and taking backward steps for another half an hour (30 minutes).

The brunette soon leads him over to where they would be stepping out on the ice and she instructed for him to hold on to the handrails so he would not fall over. He watched as she showed him how to move his feet one in front of the other.

Then he was to follow exactly what she did and he did them almost to perfection which made his shout in excitement.

This caused his teacher to giggle at how cute he looked. Soleil could not take his eyes off of the gorgeous woman in front of him.

The confidence and grace she exuded when she was in her element, he so badly wished that she would be able to be like this all the time, especially at the castle.

He knew that deep down that's all she wanted, however, something was holding her back and he so badly wanted to help her but he would not put any pressure.

Being shaken out of his thoughts, he looked down and met a pair of chocolate coloured eyes that sparkled with joy.

"Are y-you okay?"

"Yeah, I just got lost in thought."

"Oh, alright. Do you want to try and move without the guide rails?"

"Yes please."

Taking his hand, she slowly pulled him away from the walls that surrounded the rink and further out, closer to the middle so that in case he fell, his face would not smash again metal.

Still keeping hold of his hand, they skated together at a slow pace.

Ophelia giggled slightly whenever the older man stumbled slightly, but thankfully he never fell and that made her happy.

After about twenty-five (25) minutes of just slowly making their way around the entire space, she suggested he try without her holding him.

Soleil agreed and reluctantly let go of her hand, watching as she gracefully sped away to give him a little room.

Sliding one (1) foot forward, he started a nice momentum and was going pretty good for about five (5) seconds, then he went down on his ass.

"OW! SON OF A BITCH!"

"Are you o-okay?"

"Yeah, my ass is just bruised."

"Hahahahah!"

10

"OW! SON OF A BITCH!"

"Are you o-okay?"

"Yeah, my ass is just bruised."

"Hahahahah!"

For the last couple (2) of days, Soleil was not allowed back on the ice because he actually did in fact slightly bruised his tailbone.

Doctor Luke had prescribed him some pain medication in case he had any severe pain and something called a doughnut pillow.

While he was in the club's infirmary getting checked out, he was visited by Quinn, who nearly died from laughter after he found out what happened to his best friend.

Since that event, the blonde man had been ignoring him because that was so mean.

Currently, he was laying on one (1) of the lounge chairs near the pool on his pillow to keep any pressure off of his injury.

Ophelia had gone swimming about five (5) minutes before the older man had come out to the back.

The moment she saw him turn the corner, her face blushed bright red and she actually regretted the swim outfit she had put on because it was not the cutest thing on the planet.

Her outfit consisted of an orchid coloured rashguard and her pants were a charcoal shade.

She unconsciously sank further into the water so that he could only see her head and the tips of her shoulders.

To the Irishman, she could be wearing a trash bag and still look breathtakingly beautiful.

Looking up from his phone, Soleil waved at her and smiled in her direction. He watched as she slowly waded through the water closer to him and then propped her arms upon the ledge of the swimming pool.

"H-how are you feeling?"

"Lia, I'm okay. Stop worrying so much and also stop blaming yourself, it was not your fault whatsoever."

"B-but, it is. I should h-have known."

"Shush, I'm not mad at you and no, you wouldn't have known that."

"Ughhhh, f-fine."

The blonde watched in amusement as the brunette rolled her eyes and turned to dive back under the chlorinated water.

Waving goodbye before she did, he yelled a farewell in her direction and then got up to go take a warm bath with some Epsom salts.

Later that day, closer to dinner time, Ophelia found herself outside of her friend, Lyra's door and before she could knock, the door swung open.

A mop of curly locks popped up in front of her and the younger woman watched in amusement as the other woman frantically brushed her hair out of her eyes.

"Hey, honey! What brings you by?"

"I just wanted to ask you something.."

"Of course, what's up?"

Nova's mother leaned against the frame of her door and looked at her friend with concern visible all over her face.

The Hispanic woman looked down at her feet as she was scared that her question might trigger some horrible memories for her.

"I-I was wondering how were you not afraid of m-men after what happened to you before you came to the c-club? I'm sorry if that question upsets you, you don't have to answer!"

"It's quite alright, to be honest. The only reason that I could think of was that I was angrier than anything else. I was upset with Vinnie because he took away something precious to me as well as treated my daughter as if she was nothing. On top of that, he planned to sell her off to the highest bidder, so I guess I channelled that fear into anger and I was free of that rage when I slit his throat. I am not saying you should do that however, I did that because it was war and I knew how Elias felt about Nova."

Nodding, she thanked her for her wisdom, for sharing her story and as well for her time. Bidding goodbye, Ophelia made her way back down to the first (1st) floor and into the kitchen.

A few minutes later, Soleil and Reece came running through the doorway.

The pair looked like they had something mischievous up their sleeves which had the young woman instinctively grabbed a metal pot spoon in case she needed to slap her sibling. Her eyes narrowed as her brother started inching closer to her.

Almost immediately, she swung the kitchen utensil up in the air and slammed it down into his arm. She watched with an immense amount of satisfaction as her brother dramatically fell to the floor and started clutching his arm, right where she hit him.

"MAN DOWN! MAN DOWN! SUNSHINE, GO ON WITHOUT ME!"

The rest of the chefs and waiters in the kitchen stared at the trio (3) with amused smiles spread across their faces.

Before any of them could ask what was happening, Elias walked in, stopping mid-stride and just stared at everyone with a raised eyebrow.

"Why is my head chef on the floor screaming? Also, why does my head pâtissier have a pot spoon aimed at her brother?"

Shrugging, Ophelia placed the metal scoop back onto to the hook it was hanging from before and crossed her arms while glaring at her sibling.

Soleil chuckled and explained to everyone that Reece was going to cuddle her, while he was gonna beg her to make the brownies.

"You two (2) could have just asked her."

"Eliiiiiii, my arm hurts!"

"Well, that is your fault and yours alone."

Giggling, the brunette woman made her way around everyone and to the refrigerator to grab an icepack.

Reid, her brother's boyfriend tossed a hand towel to her, she stooped in front of the drama king and placed it on his arm.

"Here you go, you big baby."

"Thank you."

"I'll go make you guys some brownies, Reece."

The pair cheered and started jumping around the kitchen like a troop of kangaroos before they were dragged out into the living room by their King.

Smiling, she turned back to continue mixing the batter.

After dinner was called and everyone had eaten, the quartet dashed over to the kitchen to eat some of Ophelia's delicious confections. The couple thanked her for making it for them and bid the other pair goodnight.

Soleil turned all of his attention to the Hispanic woman and waved her over to sit next to him by the island. He still had to sit on his little doughnut pillow which made her giggle at how cute he looked.

"W-what's up?"

"I just wanted to hang out with you, Lia."

"R-really?"

"Of course, I love spending time with you."

"I-I love s-spending time with y-you too."

The two (2) of them spent the remainder of the night chatting, joking and getting to know each other even more.

It was by far the best time they had ever had in their entire lives and neither of them wanted it to end, but they both were getting extremely tired.

Soleil walked her to her room before he went to his own and plopped onto his bed, the grin that was plastered across his face the entire night.

All he could think about was the way that her brown eyes sparkled with excitement when she spoke about something she loved.

Her smile lit up the entire castle and don't get him started on the way that she looked at him, it made him want to melt into a puddle of goo.

The blonde was broken out of his inner musings by his phone ringing.

"What's up, Cillian?"

"Soleil, I've gotten an even bigger lead."

This had him flying off of his bed and he started pacing around his room.

"Really!?"

"Yes, it's taken me all the way back to Puerto Rico, I've had to ask for help from the local gangs to find out what happened."

"What have you gotten so far?"

"Catalina and Dante Diaz were both well-respected surgeons before one of their patients had passed away due to complications during surgery. He was the head of the Puerto Rican Mafia but also was seventy-eight (78) years old. After that, the couple along with their first (1st) child were forced to flee as they were receiving death threats."

Running his hands through his hair, the Irishman's already pale skin got even lighter as he felt all of the blood drain from his face.

This was getting more complicated by the second and he was not sure if he wanted to hear the rest.

"Does it get worst?"

"Yes."

"Oh my."

"A year (1) after they fled to Sweden, Catalina fell pregnant with Ophelia and for fourteen (14) years they were able to lay low. However, someone found out about their new location and then they were forced to abandon their kids. Before they could get out of the country, they were caught and taken back to their home country. Which is where they are now and that's how far I have gotten."

Blowing out a large breath, Soleil was in shock and he could not fully comprehend what he was actually being told.

Cillian had gone out of his way to look into this, but not only is his wedding coming up but his life could potentially be put in danger.

"Please, be careful and if it gets too dangerous, abandon it. That information should be enough to let them know that their parents still loved them and did not want to leave. It's not worth risking your life."

"I promise you I will. I gotta go."

"Bye, Cilly."

"Bye, Solar System."

11

"Please, be careful and if it gets too dangerous, abandon it. That information should be enough to let them know that their parents still loved them and did not want to leave. It's not worth risking your life."

"I promise you I will. I gotta go."

"Bye, Cilly."

"Bye, Solar System."

It had been about a week (1) since Soleil had received any updates from Cillian and as worried as he was becoming, he knew he could not just try to get into contact with him.

The figure skating lessons were proving to be a very welcomed distraction.

Since he was given the all-clear by Doctor Luke about six (6) days ago, he had been dragged back onto the ice by Ophelia, who was a lot stronger than she actually looked. Since then he had perfected his balance and the basic movements.

Currently, he was watching his instructor perform a move known as the axel jump and was expected to learn it as well.

The blonde had questioned why he needed to know such advanced moves for what he was doing this for and this was the response he got.

"I l-look up your sister, Dinah and she obsessed with f-figure skating. So, I'm covering a-all the bases."

"For some reason, I feel like she's related to you and not me. Lia, you literally thought of the fact she more than likely will want to go over the top, as she usually does."

"Exactly, so let's c-continue, we have an hour (1) l-left."

Nodding, he watched as she gracefully got into the start position and carefully demonstrated from the beginning to end on how to do this specific move.

After a couple (2) more viewings, it was Soleil's turn to try in sections.

Step one (1) was to stand still with his feet shoulder-width apart, hold it for a few minutes and then repeat so he could get comfortable with it.

Then, he was instructed by the brunette woman to put his arms out to his sides and let them sit there, without moving yet.

"Okay, perfect! Bring your ankles about six (6) inches (15 cm) apart and tense them. Next, bring your ankles in closer together under your body as if you are trying to squeeze a ball between them. This will help you to increase your speed as you skate. Tense the muscles in your ankles as you bring them together to help prepare yourself for the jump. DON'T MOVE TILL I TELL YOU!"

This made the Irishman jump as she yelled at him when he shifted slightly and this made him realise this was the first (1st) time she had had ever raised her voice at him.

Seconds later, he also noticed she had not stuttered, which he concluded was probably because she was in the zone.

Ophelia skated forward to be directly in front of him and he watched with a mixture of surprise and pride on his face as she touched him to position him for the third (3rd) step. The blonde listened as she gave a tip for this part.

"Proper body alignment is crucial for successfully executing an axel. Practice your stance until it feels like second nature. This will help to ensure that you maintain the correct stance during your axels, got that?"

Nodding, the pair skated through the rest of the sections and before either of them knew it, they only had ten (10) minutes left before they had to leave.

Clapping her little hands together, Ophelia asked if he would like to and try a full attempt on the axel jump.

"Yes!"

Giggling, she gave him some room and wiped her sweaty hands, she was feeling rather anxious because the last thing she wanted for him to get to hurt again. She decided it was best for the two (2) of them if she gave a countdown to calm his nerves.

"3, 2 and 1, go!"

Her brown eyes watched nervously as he got into the starting stance and performed the steps that came after.

All of them were done to the utmost perfection and then came the part she was dreading, the actual jumping part.

It flew by so fast that she almost had not caught it. She watched in absolute amazement as Soleil landed gracefully, facing the opposite direction than when he had begun.

He glided back on his left foot and put his arms down to stabilise himself.

Letting a loud squeal, Ophelia shed her timidness for a second and literally flew into the Irishman's arms.

He stumbled back slightly as she crashed into him, but managed to catch his balance before they hit the frozen floor.

He was shocked, to say the least, but the Hispanic woman did another thing that caught him off guard.

She kissed him.

On the cheek.

Near his mouth.

As quickly as she had gotten there, she was gone. He watched frozen as he tried to process what just happened as the brunette skated to the edge of the rink and got out. She removed her figure skates and practically jumped into her sneakers.

Without looking back at him, she ran out of the building. Breaking out his stupor, the blonde followed her but by the time he got outside, he was watching her car peel out of the parking lot and disappear.

It had been a couple (2) of hours since Ophelia had pecked the Irishman on his cheek and since he had gotten back to the Odin's Riders castle, he had yet to see her. The brunette was avoiding him and he knew it.

The logical explanation was that because of her crippling fear of men, she had realised what she had done and ran off to hide.

Unfortunately for him, that ugly part of his subconscious came out to play at this very moment.

It kept telling him that she ran away because she regretted jumping into his arms, feeling his body against hers and hated the kiss that she had planted on his cheek.

Every time he thought about it, the spot where her lips were pressed so sweetly against his skin, burned with the fire of a thousand (1000) suns.

Running his hand through his blonde locks, Soleil released a heavy sigh.

He knew those reasons were bullshit, but he still could not help but believe them slightly. Was he really that repulsive to her?

As if he could spider-sense that something was wrong with his son, the Irishman's father, Haru called.

(Haru is a name that originated from the Japanese language. Haru means 'light, 'sun' or 'clear weather'.)

"Hey, Dadaí."

('Dadaí' is the Irish word for 'Father' in English.)

"Don't 'hey, Dadaí' me."

"What? Why?"

He could almost hear his father rolling his grey eyes into the back of his head, just as he normally would do when he was exasperated.

"I'm your father. I know when something is wrong with you."

"Uh, Dadaí that's a bit creepy. I thought that was something Athair would say."

('Athair is the Irish Gaelic word for 'Father' in English.)

(Yes, Soleil has two (2) fathers as his parents.)

"Both of us say that. It's just that he says it more often than I! Anyways, are you okay?"

Blowing out a breath, he replied to his father, explaining to him the entire situation between him and Ophelia.

At the end of it, he felt his eyes start to well up with unshed tears, as he finally released all that pent of emotions.

In the background on his Dadaí's end, he could hear his Athair walk into whatever room he was in and ask him, who he was on the phone with.

The second he heard that it was their son, you could practically hear Haru be thrown aside as Auberon tackled him for the phone.

(Auberon also spelt as Oberon is the 'large moon of Uranus, named after the King of Fairies in Shakespeare's Midsummer Night's Dream.')

"MY BABY BOY! HOW ARE YOU!?"

"H-hi, Athair..."

Soleil had tried to bite back his sobs, but he knew that both of his fathers could hear his voice quivering.

Before he could react, the audio call changed to a Facetime one, so he grabbed his laptop, flung it open and answered.

Immediately two (2) very concerned faces popped up on his screen. Haru's grey orbs were filled with worry as he ran his hands through his bright red hair in distress.

While Auberon was also looking quite concerned, his sea-green and baby blue eyes were filled with protectiveness.

(Auberon has heterochromia, meaning he has a birth defect caused by Waardenburg Syndrome or another syndrome.)

"Is there someone bothering you!?"

"W-what? Athair, no! Dadaí, explain to him!"

Soleil listened as his Dad relayed the story to him and watched as his other parent slumped in his chair in surprise. Suddenly, both their heads snapped in his direction and they chuckled at him.

"Why are you guys laughing?"

"Son, you're overreacting. From what you told your father and me understand why she reacted as she did. Ophelia seems to like you but may not know how to handle that feeling because of whatever may have happened to her and with her doing that earlier at practice, it more than likely caused her to feel embarrassed."

"Basically what your Dadaí is saying is, you're a drama king, baby boy."

Rolling his eyes, Soleil muttered, "Geez, thanks, Athair."

After speaking to his fathers for a few more minutes, the blonde man soon hung up and fell back onto his bed.

Closing his eyes, his mind was soon consumed filled with thoughts of what if she actually didn't she like him as he drifted off quickly.

Elsewhere in the giant castle, said woman was having a similar talk with Lyra, her older brother, Reece and his boyfriend, Reid. The trio (3) was hanging out in the waiter's room when there was a knock on the door.

Getting up from the his place on the bed, the Swedish young man slipped off his bed after pecking his lover on the lips and made his way over to the door. Opening, he could not hide his surprise to see Ophelia standing there, looking out of breath.

"Oph? Are you okay? Your face is bright red!"

Hearing that his little sister was not looking too hot, the Hispanic male flew off the bed and softly grabbed her face.

Brown eyes scanning her face to see if she was not feeling well, just as he thought she was coming down with the cold or something, he caught a flash of sadness.

"Ophbear, what happened? I know you were supposed to be at the skating rink with Sol."

"W-well, everything was going fine until the last ten (10) minutes of the lesson. I was so nervous about him performing an attempt on the axel j-jump, but when he actually landed it perfectly, I got so excited....that I...."

Raising their eyebrows, the three (3) of them stared at her waiting to hear what she did after he finished the move. Reid made a motion with his hand to signal for her to get a move on with the tale.

"Well...I...uh...I skated over to him and jumped into his arms. Then I kissed him on the cheek...near his lips.."

It felt like thousands (1000s) of years before anyone had said anything after the truth left her lips and just as she was going to say something, the brunette was interrupted.

The first (1st) person to scream was Lyra and then the other two (2) followed.

Ophelia's eyes widened as she stared at them as if they had lost their minds. Raising her arms, she started waving for them to stop.

"What is wrong with you guys!?"

"What!? Nothing!"

"Then why are you screaming like a set of banshees?"

"Honey, you literally kissed him! What happened after that?"

Nova's mother watched as the younger woman's expression fell from her face and her eyes welled up slightly. Narrowing his eyes, Reece placed his hands on his sibling's face forcing her to look up at him.

"Ophelia Aurelia Elena Diaz, did you run away from him without explaining a thing?"

"Maybe..."

Groaning loudly, the trio (3) started yelling why did she do that which made poor Ophelia feel even more guilty than she already was feeling.

Footsteps sounded coming down the hallway and soon Nova arrived in front of the group.

"Maybe you three (3) should stop yelling at the poor girl and realise that she's crying."

"Ophbear, I'm sorry."

"I-It's okay. I'm going to go to my r-room, see you guys later."

With that said, she turned on her heel and walked away quickly. The second the Hispanic woman turned the corner, the unshed tears started streaming down her cheeks.

Wiping them away, she rushed into her bedroom and slammed the door, locking it after.

Sliding down with her back pressed against the wooden entrance, she released the heartwrenching sobs that she was holding back.

Wrapping her arms around herself, she whimpered, "Why can't I be normal?"

Further down the hall back at Reid's bedroom, Nova was yelling at everyone of them, including her mother for how insensitive they were being.

Glaring at Reece, who flinched back at her icy gaze, she reprimided him for forgetting everything she had went through.

"I'm fucking disappointed in all of you, but especially you, Reece. You know better than anyone else that she reacted the way she did because of that!"

Once she was finished with her rant, she huffed and stormed off. The brunette was heartbroken for the way he acted, he wanted to protect his friend but in turn he hurt his baby sister's feelings without realising it.

Just as he was about to runoff, Lyra grabbed his arm and shook her head at him. She explained that Ophelia needed time to cool off and they should leave her be. They could apologise to her later when she was ready.

A couple (2) hours later, Soleil was woken up from his nap by an incessant ringing. Groaning, he flipped over and grabbed his phone, his eyebrows furrowed in confusion at the unknown number that was calling.

"Hello, who is this?"

"It's Cillian, you ass."

"How the fuck would I know that? You're calling from an unknow number, which brings me to my next question, where the fuck have you been?"

"I broke my phone a while back so I haven't been able to get into contact with you, plus I was drowning in the work for this case. However, I do have very good news for you."

"I'm listening."

What came next had the blonde man flying out of his bed and pacing his room.

"Are you serious?"

"Very."

12

"Are you serious?"

"Very."

Soleil could not believe what he was hearing, it was absolutely insane and sounded as if it had come straight out of a fictional book.

"I'm on my way to Sweden right now, Solar System."

"Why?"

"I'm delivering the surprise to you for you to give it to them because, at the end of the day, you were the one who was deadset on finding them."

"Okay, but explain to me exactly what the fuck went down during the week (1) you had been gone and why the fucking hell you did not get into contact with me earlier. Did you think about if something happened to you and I could not get to you? How would Dinah feel if you just went missing because of me? She'd be devastated, you are her WORLD!"

The blonde man let out an exasperated sigh as he sank back down onto his bed and rubbed his temples with his free hand.

He knew that he was the one (1) to have enlisted his brother-in-law's help, but like he had told him, if it became too dangerous, abandon it.

"I know, I'm sorry, but I was in deep at that point and I did not want to go contacting you in case something triggered them."

"Who the fuck is them?"

"The Puerto Rican Mafia."

"WHAT?!!!"

His grey orbs were opened to the size of saucers when he heard those four (4) words travel through the receiver of his cellphone.

"Yeah, I got into contact with them when I was buying some groceries. I ended up being allowed to request a meeting with the current Don of the family and went from there."

"You're lying to me."

"H-how did you know that?"

"I'm not stupid, but apparently you fucking are, now what the fuck actually went down, Cillian."

The ginger male sighed and ran his hands through his shoulder-length hair, he was hoping that his brother-in-law would just brush the details, but obviously, he was wrong.

Reaching into the overhead cabin, he grabbed his briefcase.

Entering the access code, he took out the secured documents and files that he had compiled during the week he went ghost.

Flipping to the exact page that he was looking for, he started to explain to the blonde man on the phone.

The trail that he had found had gone cold not long after he had gotten to Puerto Rico and he had spent restless hours looking for something, anything.

One (1) day he was on his way back to his hotel when he was cornered by a group of men and you could tell they were not from the legal side of town.

They gave him two (2) options, either come with them peacefully or allow them to use force, even though they had already kind of did.

Cillian opted to go with the course of action that did not end up with him shot in the head and his body thrown in a shallow ditch.

He was gagged, his limbs were bound and his sight was covered, all he could hear was Spanish being spoken along with cars driving by.

Being roughly thrown into the back of a van was not something he had planned on happening, but at this point, he really did not have a choice.

Once they arrived at their destination, a pair of hands had grabbed him and dragged him out the drunk to the door.

Soon his mouth and eyes were freed, that was when he realised he was sitting before the current head of the Puerto Rican Mafia.

Flashback to One (1) week ago.

"Hola mi amigo. Parece que mis hombres te han traído a mí."

('Hola mi amigo. Parece que mis hombres te han traído a mí.' translated from Spanish to English is, 'Hello my friend. It seems my men have brought you to me.')

"Yo, no hablo español."

('Yo, no hablo español.' translated from Spanish to English is, 'I don't speak English.')

Laughter erupted throughout the room as apparently to them, what Cillian said was downright hilarious.

As he looked around, he saw that many of them were bending over with their hands placed on their knees as they wheezed for air.

"My friend, thank you for giving us some of the worst Español that we have ever heard. However, you see, my men brought you to our lovely home for a special reason. Do you know what it is?"

"No, but I'm sure you're about to tell me."

This caused the playful smirk to slip off the Hispanic man's tanned face and a deathly glare quickly replaced it.

Internally, the redhead smirked, he was going to rile him up if needed and let him get sloppy. He was also establishing that he was not going to be threatened.

"Well, mi amigo, seem's like you have a bit of a defiant streak in you, but that's not a problema because that makes things all the more exhilarating."

Rolling his cedar coloured orbs, he told the slightly older man to hurry up and get on with what he wanted to tell him.

The leader, Javier's left eye twitched in annoyance but he gripped the arm of his chair and held back his anger, wanting to let it out on his victim later.

"You are here because word around town is you have been snooping around looking for any information that you could get your little grubby hands on. There was one (1) problem though was that you were so very sloppy."

It was Cillian's turn to practically fall over as he let out booming laughter, by the time the two (2) heavily tattooed men that were guarding the door came to hoist him back up, he had tears streaming down his pale cheeks.

"Are you sure about that? My job is being a private investigator if I wanted to have stayed hidden, you have never found me out."

"Fuck you, puta. Lleva a este hombre al sótano."

('Lleva a este hombre al sótano.' translated from Spanish to English is, 'Take this man to the basement.')

Realising that if he did not act now, they would take him away and he would more than likely never been seen or heard from again.

The ginger knew there was no going back now and it there was only one way out.

"I know what you want."

Those five (5) words had the Don stopping in his tracks near the doorway and him turning on his heel. Javier stooped directly in front of the Irishman and narrowed his eyes. Forcefully grabbing his jaw, he made their eyes meet.

"You don't know shit."

"I do actually, I know that you are actively searching for Carmin Leigh and her daughter, Maya Leigh or should I said, Maya Morales. See, both of those women were kidnapped from you, by a rival gang, yes?"

Turning to his men behind him, the noirette told them to get out and make sure no one bothered them unless he said so or it was urgent.

Once they left, he freed Cillian's hands from his bounds with the promise that he'd kill him where he stood if he tried anything.

"What do you know?"

"I know everything and I also know where they are being held."

"GIVE ME THE INFORMATION NOW!"

"No. I have something you want and you have something I want."

"What could you possibly want?"

"Catalina and Dante Diaz."

Cillian watched as the azure blue eyes widened in shock as he heard two (2) names that no one ever even dared to utter after they were brought back home.

"Why do you want them?"

"Your people caused them to flee their hometown and leave their practice. They also caused them to live in constant fear for fifteen (15) years after and then have them abandon their two (2) children."

"THEY KILLED MY FATHER!"

"Sebastian Pedro Marco Morales died of complications due to surgery. Your father's advisor was informed that the surgery would be very risky because of his age along with his previously diagnosed health conditions. However, he forced them to perform the procedure and even though they had tried to save him, they could not. Unfortunately them, he lied and told you that they murdered him because he did not want to take the blame for making them do it."

He watched as the information settled into Don's mind and watched as a look of determination crossed his face.

"Let's make a deal. You stay for a week (1) to help me find my wife and daughter, then you can have the doctors. I'll clear their debts to us and they will be free to go."

"Deal."

End of Flashback.

Soleil sucked in a breath as he listened to the way the older man was treated and he could not help but feel a wave of guilt wash over him.

The blonde is the one (1) who put him in this situation and so many things could have gone wrong.

The pair talked for a few minutes longer, just catching up on everything that was currently happened along with how the Diaz parents were doing.

Apparently, they were holding up really well and extremely grateful for being rescued.

Cillian also told the blonde that he had not informed them of where they were going and who they were going to go see.

The pair wanted it to be a surprise for both of the groups and after they discussed a few other things, they said their goodbyes.

"I'll see you in less than fifteen (15) hours, talk to you later. I need to sleep."

"Sleep for the majority of it, but make sure to eat. See you soon, Cilly."

"See you soon, Solar System."

13

"I'll see you in less than fifteen (15) hours, talk to you later. I need to sleep."

"Sleep for the majority of it, but make sure to eat. See you soon, Cilly."

"See you soon, Solar System."

Waking up early was not something that Soleil was fond of doing but for the occasion that was taking place today, he needed to.

Elias and Nova had driven to the airport to pick up their three (3) guests, however, Cillian was only staying for a day to rest, then on his way back to Ireland.

After the blonde finished brushing his teeth, his phone pinged with a text message from his King saying that they had arrived and were going to take them to get settled. He sent a text back letting him know that he'll send the signal when they're ready.

Setting down his phone on the marbled counter of his bathroom sink, he switched out his earrings for one's that he had recently bought along with his rings.

Brushing the tangles out of his hair, he fixed his leather jacket and made his way out of the room.

His first (1st) stop was Reece's room because he still was slightly apprehensive at seeing his friend's younger sister after what happened at their last lesson.

His fathers' words rang through his head as he walked down the hallway but the nasty part of subconscious also resurfaced.

Little did he know that the older male also was dancing around seeing his sibling after what had occurred last night.

The Irishman soon saw the familiar door that was painted a navy blue with a giant 'Catalina Blue' that was recently painted on it in memory of his mother, who was named after the flower.

Raising his fist, he was in the midst of knocking when the door was flung open and he accidentally hit Reece in the middle of his forehead.

This caused the shorter man to let out a loud yelp and slapped his hand over where he was injured.

"What was that for!?"

"I didn't know you were about to open the door like an idiot. How the fuck did you know I was outside?"

"I did not! I thought you were Ophbear."

Giving him a puzzled look, he quickly noticed something. Narrowing his grey eyes, Soleil bent forward at the waist to look into the Hispanic man's eyes. He saw that the brunette was fidgeting and refusing to meet his gaze.

"What did you do?"

"Let's talk about it later, was there something you needed?"

Internally sighing, the blonde rolled his eyes and decided to let it go for now as he had more important matters that needed both Diaz children. He explained that he had something to show him and Ophelia.

Gesturing for him to follow him, the Irishman made his way over to the stairway all the while his friend was pestering him about what he was going to show them.

Ignoring the man's whining, he made his way down to the floor below them where the other brunette slept.

Coming up to her orchid coloured door, he knocked and this time he actually managed to do it without hitting someone in the face again. Rocking nervously back on his heels, he waited for her to answer.

Reece was hiding behind his friend as he was not sure if his sister saw him that she would want to go.

He had a feeling the second (1) she caught a glimpse of her brother, she would slam the door in both of their faces.

Soleil shook his head at the older man's antics but did not even try to question it and not long after he did that, he heard rustling coming from behind the door. A couple (2) of seconds later, a familiar pair of chocolate brown eyes were peering up at him.

"Hey, Lia."

"H-hey, Sol, is everything o-okay?"

"Yeah, but I need you to go get ready because I need to show you and your brother something."

"O-okay, please c-come in and wait."

Thanking her, he watched as she stepped aside to let him in and with slight amusement as her eyes became wide when she saw her older sibling. Reece shyly waved at her and ducked into her bedroom without a word.

Both men sat on her bed as she went about grabbing her clothes from her wardrobe and then scurried into the sanctuary that was her bathroom.

Once the door was closed, she leaned her back against it and blew out a breath of relief.

Ophelia was glad that Soleil did not seem to look upset about yesterday but she was slightly worried about how nonchalant he was acting.

Did this mean that he did not like her? The slight prospect of that alone was enough to bring tears to her eyes.

Wiping them away, she shook her head to clear her mind of negative thoughts and stood up straight. Looking at herself in the mirror, she smiled brightly and whispered quietly, "You've got this!"

After her miniature pep talk, the brunette hopped into the shower, grabbing her favourite body wash which was blue fig and orange blossom scented.

Lathering it up, she carefully cleaned her body and made sure to shave anywhere that needed to be.

Outside in her bedroom, the blonde had flopped back onto her bed and was now laying down with his eyes closed.

He was lost in thought, thinking about how the pair would react to seeing their parents for the first time in over eight (8) years.

He silently prayed to Odin that they would not be upset with Cillian and him for digging into their past to find them. The Irishman was broken out of his musings by Reece poking him in his ribcage.

"Ow! What!"

"Are you okay?"

"Yeah, why?"

"You look extremely exhausted, did you get enough sleep last night?"

Humming, Soleil knew he could not lie and say he was not tired because even after he had hung up on Cillian, he was unable to go back to sleep.

The information that he had received had honestly kept him up all night.

"Nah, I did not, but it's okay."

Before his friend could open his mouth to reply, the bathroom door opened and the scent of orange blossoms permeated throughout the room.

Ophelia stepped out and it took every single ounce of sheer self-control and will power for the blonde man not to pull her into his arms.

She looked absolutely gorgeous in her apricot coloured sundress with was decorated with tiny white flowers.

The puffed capped sleeves showcased her shoulders and framed her collar-bones while the end of the dress had a slight frill to it.

Her dainty hands were holding a pair of white mini wedged heels and her cellphone. Clearing her throat, the Hispanic woman watched with a slight blush on her face as the Irishman's grey orbs snapped up to meet her gaze.

A light pink blush dusted his pale cheeks as he realised he was caught doing a full body check out on her, but he really could not help it.

She was a goddess in every sense of the word to him and despite what happened the day before, no one could take her place.

Once she had strapped on her shoes, the trio (3) made their way out of her room and to the elevator.

As they waited for the elevator to call, Soleil took out his phone from his back pocket and shot a text to Nova letting them know they were on their way.

Immediately he received a text back saying that Catalina and Dante were in the private gazebo of the garden.

Smiling, he put his phone away as the elevator dinged and the doors swooshed open. They all got in and he pressed the button that would carry them to the ground floor.

Getting out of the elevator, they were met by Elias and Nova, who gave them all hugs. Leading them out back and through the secret path in the garden that was framed by cherry blossom trees, they stopped right before the belvedere came into view.

"Lia and Reese's Pieces close your eyes please."

"O-okay."

"Alright."

The Diaz siblings closed their eyes and allowed themselves to be steered into whatever direction they were going.

Soon they were halted and told to open their eyes. Soleil watched as the pair opened their eyes and met the sight of their parents, who they thought were dead.

Their brown eyes welled up with tears as they could not believe what they were seeing. The other three (3) patted them on their shoulders and whispered, "We'll leave you four (4) alone to talk."

"M-Mom? D-Dad?"

"Its good to see you both my beautiful children."

"YOU'RE ALIVE?!"

"Yes, Reece mi hijo."

14

"M-Mom? D-Dad?"

"Its good to see you both my beautiful children."

"YOU'RE ALIVE?!"

"Yes, Reece mi hijo."

The Diaz siblings still could not believe the sight that was placed before them.

The people who sat before them still looked the same as they did when they had left eight (8) years ago, just a little more wrinkles sat on their caramel skin.

Catalina's walnut tresses were peppered with grey strands due to the immense stress that seemed to have gone under since the last time they had seen their mother. Dante's once charcoal locks were now more salt than pepper and he looked weary.

Ophelia took a tentative step forward as she looked into the eyes that were so similar to hers and her brother's.

A hand was placed on her shoulder, looking back at Reece, he gave her a supportive smile, letting her know that she was not alone.

Deep down, the Hispanic male knew that she was the one (1) who was most affected by their parents' disappearance as around that time, that was when she needed them the most.

He felt bad because, during the hardest days of her life, he could barely be there as he was trying to keep them afloat with work.

Somedays, he wished he could turn the clocks back so that he could warn the younger version of himself about how badly his sister's condition would worsen.

Looking into her eyes, he saw a lot of pain, agony and fear lurking within the depths.

He knew the questions that were swimming along inside of her thoughts, like what if they are just here to say goodbye for good? Or if they really did not want them anymore?

It was hard for them to understand what was happening and why the pair returned now.

"Mi hijo y mi hija, por favor, vengan y siéntense."

('Mi hijo y mi hija, por favor, vengan y siéntense.' translates from Spanish to English as 'My son and daughter, please come and sit down.')

Frowning slightly, Ophelia took hold of her brother's thin hand and walked with him over to where the older couple (2) sat under the gazebo.

Taking the adjacent seats near the table, the siblings stared at them with questioning gazes that demanded answers.

Sighing, Catalina looked down at her wrinkled hands and twisted the silver wedding band nervously. She knew that her children wanted answers because of everything that happened and how suddenly they left.

"Creo que es hora de que ustedes dos sepan la verdad."

('Creo que es hora de que ustedes dos sepan la verdad.' translates from Spanish to English as 'I think it's time for you two (2) to know the truth.')

"I think it's been long overdue, mother."

Back inside of the castle, Soleil had just finished chatting with Nova and Elias about how they thought their friends were fairing with their parents.

He was now making his way up the stairs to the floor where Cillian was currently resting.

He wanted to check up on his brother in law as he did not get the chance to when he woke up and his mind was worried about his physical being.

Moreso, his mental wellbeing as he normally was not put into situations of danger like what he had just gone through.

Knocking on the door, he heard an immediate muffled, "Come on in, the door is open." Pushing open the door, he saw that his fellow Irishman was laying on his bed, facing the ceiling. Looking over, Cillian smiled softly at the younger man.

"Hey, Solar System."

"Oh stop, but hey, Cilly. How are you feeling?"

The redhead gingerly sat up and tried to hide his wince as his injuries were still killing him. The blonde noticed this immediately and rushed over to his friend. Helping him up the rest of the way, a look of concern washed over his pale face.

"What happened that you haven't told me?"

"When they threw me in the trunk I hit my back and they punched me in the gut for good measure."

"Did you not get any medical treatment?"

"Um, no."

Running a hand through his golden locks, he muttered a frustrated, "Mac soith."

('Mac soith.' translated from Irish to English is, 'Son of a bitch.')

Smiling sheepishly, Cillian explained that his plan was to stay and rest for one (1) day in Sweden, then hop onto a flight back to home. The only thing was that the younger man was not supposed to find out he had gotten injured.

This caused Soleil to lightly slap him upside his head and scold him for trying to something so reckless.

He informed him that he was staying for at least a couple (2) more days so he could be checked out by a doctor and rest some more.

"W-WHAT? NO! I CAN'T!"

"Would you rather face Dinah and have her realise that you got injured because you were crazy."

This caused the older man to start to heavily sweat and internally panic as he thought about all the ways his lovely fiance would most likely kill him.

Women that came from the Walsh clan were a force to be reckoned with and one you did not want to antagonise for good reason.

Unlike most of the old money families that were known for patriarchal heads, Soleil's lineage was strictly matriarchal from the very start, with the exception of his parents.

The oldest female would take over as the matron after she got married and had her first (1st) child.

The blonde was proud of his familial traditions, but oftentimes it left all the men in the clan absolutely terrified.

His grandmother was still the reigning head since she never had any girls and soon it would be passed down to his sister, which meant, everyone run for their lives.

"Rethink your life decisions and choices now?"

"Shut up, Solar System, but yes."

"Good idea, but the topic of discussing how petrifying Dinah is was not the reason I came here to see you. I wanted to check up on you, physically, which I can tell is not okay, but also mentally. I put you on a job that took you into dangerous waters and that's not what you are used to."

Resting his hand on the younger man's shoulder, Cillian shook his head slightly as he knew the other was projecting all the blame onto himself.

He knew what he was doing and what he was walking into when he agreed to help, he needed to let him know that.

The ginger reassured him that mentally he was okay, swore up and down that he saw nothing that could have possibly traumatised him at any point.

He kept reminding him that this was not the first nor last time he would have seen a gun or gotten hurt on the job.

It took about an hour of just talking it out and pure convincing to assure his brother-in-law that he was okay.

After that, the pair just sat down on the soft king size mattress and watched a bunch of youtube videos to unwind.

Outside in the back garden, under the protection of the decorated gazebo's roof, the Diaz family was engaged in a heated argument. Catalina and Dante wanted their daughter to enrol back into figure skating classes.

Reece was on his sister's side of the debate as she was not about to go back into the profession that caused her so much pain.

On top of that, she was extremely with the job and position that she had currently obtained.

"We are your parents!"

"Actually you are not, remember you signed over the rights of being her legal guardian to me, plus she's also fucking twenty-two (22) years old."

Ophelia leaned back into her seat with a large smug smile on her face as she let her older brother take the reins.

She was extremely happy to know they were alive and the real reason for their sudden departure from their lives.

However, that did not mean that the couple could just start to boss them around and dictate their lives as if they had a right to.

She knew that her brother agreed with her on this, the pair wanted their parents to be a part of their family again.

Rolling her chocolate brown orbs, she slammed her palms face down onto the clothed table and glared at the two (2) that were sitting across from her.

This action caused the other three (3) to pause their bickering and look at her with eyes filled with shock.

"You have no right to try to order me around. Listen, both of us are glad to see you but we lived without you for over eight (8) fucking years, we can go the rest of our days just as easy. If you want to be in our lives like you say do, then you need to fucking realise that we are adults who can make their own decisions and choose their careers without your help. You need to fucking accept that otherwise, you can leave and pretend we are fucking dead."

After finishing her miniature rant, Ophelia pushed her chair back and got up. Staring at her parents, she gave them a tight smile and her brother a gentle, reassuring one.

"Now, excuse me. There is something I need to do."

With that being said, she turned her back to them and walked away with her head held high. A large grin spread across her face as she realised that she spoke to them with a firm voice and not a shaky one.

Catalina called out to her daughter, but Reece stopped her with a raised hand and shook his head slightly.

He told his mother and father to leave her alone, to let her go do what she needed to do as he had an idea what it was.

The brunette had made her way back inside the castle and started to ask around if anyone had seen a certain blonde Irishman. One of the thralls answered her and told her that she had just seen him going into the main lounge.

Nodding and thanking her, she walked over to the doorway of the large room where she quickly spotted him. He was laying on the couch, upside down for some reason with his head hanging off.

Walking further in, she quietly called out his name and watched as his head snapped in her direction.

Grey orbs met hers and instantly both their faces were dusted pink. Soleil quickly righted himself on the chair and cleared his throat.

"W-what's up, Lia?"

"I need to talk to you."

15

"W-what's up, Lia?"

"I need to talk to you."

Sitting up even straighter, Soleil felt his panic rise at the serious tone of her voice and the fact that she did not even stutter when she spoke to him just now. Looking around, he remembered that there were other members of the club in the room.

Gathering his things, he made his way over to the Hispanic woman and asked her to join him in his room for privacy.

She nodded and followed behind him. On the outside, she was the picture-perfect representation of stoic and calm, but on the inside, her heart had dropped to her ass.

Once they reached his bedroom door, she looked up at him and finally shed her serene disposition, showing the blonde exactly how nervous she really was.

In return, he gave her what he hoped was a comforting smile and opening his door, gesturing for her to go in.

The pair got comfortable with the Hispanic woman sitting cross-legged on his king-sized bed and he was seated on his window seat.

"Soooo, what was it that you wanted to talk about, Lia?"

Fiddling with her fingers, she averted her gaze from his and explained to him that she was going to confide in him why she was so petrified of men.

Peering through her eyelashes, she saw that his face get deadly serious and also held a glimpse of concern.

"Are you sure? Lia, you do not by any means need to tell me any of this, I understand its private matter that only, Reece, Benjamin, Nova, Elias and you know about."

"I'm sure. I want y-you to know."

Getting up from his place by the window, Soleil sat back down next to the brunette to offer her any sort of nearby support.

He knew this was going to be a hard thing for her to speak about and he was beyond honoured that she was telling him but still was terribly worried.

"W-when I was fifteen (15), I h-had a stalker. I had never met h-him and still to this day I have no idea w-who he actually is. All I k-knew was he signed everything he sent with the n-name, 'Alex' and a tiny r-red heart next to it. It just randomly started a-after I had won the g-gold medal for the state championships. I had o-opened my l-locker and a folded piece of p-pink paper fell out, immediately I was alarmed because n-no one besides the s-skaters was allowed back t-there."

"You're doing amazing, Lia. Take all the time you need, okay?"

Shooting him a grateful smile, because she really was appreciative about how supportive the blonde man was. If he was not the way he was, she would not have been able to make it as far as she already had.

"W-when I opened the p-paper, it was a letter addressed to m-me and what I read made me rush to the nearest b-bin to empty my stomach. He was d-describing how beautiful my t-thighs and b-breasts looked in my costume. He also s-spoke about how much he so b-sadly wanted to reach out and c-caress my soft subtle l-looking skin. It ended with t-that and his signature that would h-haunt me even after I l-left the career I l-loved."

The Irishman did not know what to say and she seemed to not mind the silence as she looked as if she drew comfort from it.

He knew he was filled with rage and absolutely disgusted by what he had just heard, for Odin's sake, she was fifteen (15) years old!

Ophelia sucked a deep breath in and clasped her dainty hands tighter as she prepared to continue her story. She explained that ever since that day, she would receive a written letter in her locker, but it did not stay like that for long.

Soon it escalated to the point of where the notes would be found inside of her duffel back, which was locked inside of her personal cabinet.

That meant he had gotten past the locks she placed on both items and possibly went through her stuff.

Unfortunately for the young Hispanic girl at the time, this was just the beginning, things were going to take a dark and twisted turn very soon.

She was unable to change lockers with anyone and she was also too scared to let someone know what was happening in fear he hurt her.

It was not as if she could also just stop bringing her backpack with her as it held her skates, training clothes and any other extra necessities she needed for a regular day at the rink. The brunette had to play face and pretend everything was alright, but on the inside, she was dying slowly.

Her love for the competitive sport was slowly dwindling but she could not just drop out as the next five (5) years of her career were paid for already by her at the time missing parents.

She wanted to make them proud somehow and this was the only way she could have thought about at the time.

So, for the next half a decade (5) she would endure disturbing, perverted letters.

However, that was the least of the problem, because the day after her sixteenth (16) birthday, she received a wrapped box in her locker and upon opening it, she discovered he had bought her a cornflower blue lace thong.

The note that was attached to it had said, 'I can't wait to see you in this and then tear it off with my teeth, sweetheart.'

From then on, things kept escalating and getting worse.

Every day, he would send her a new piece of lingerie along with a short disturbing note.

When she turned eighteen (18) years old, she had tried to move along with her life and got a boyfriend, who would end up being the only one (1) she ever had. 'Alex' did not like that whatsoever and started to amp up his stalking.

Shortly after, she was receiving photographs of her from the same day with her friends or her significant other. They weren't ones that seemed to have been taken at a vastly far distance, but in fact, was probably taken about six (6) feet away from her or slightly further away.

The letters as well became less perverted and sexual, instead, they took a more threatening route. Sadly, she still had a couple (2) of years before she could retire and go into hiding of some sort.

Ophelia endured that torture for over five (5) years while she was a seasoned figure skater, but the minute they announced her retirement, everything came to a screeching halt.

No more notes, lingerie and photographs, but at that point the damage had already been done.

She had broken up with her boyfriend, distanced herself from her friends and barely left her home. Reece did everything for her and he had only recently found out after it all seemed to have ended. He was devastated that she went through that and even worse all by herself.

"T-that's my story."

"Oh fuck, Lia. I am so so fucking sorry. That man is a disgusting piece of shit and I want to just fucking grab him by his grimy ass neck and kill him!"

Soleil's jaw was beginning to ache at how tightly he was grinding his teeth together, but the pain he was feeling did not compare to the raging fire that was blazing in his heart.

He wanted to find this 'Alex' and rip him to shreds.

He was so lost in his revengeful thoughts that he had not noticed the brunette calling his name, but suddenly he was jolted out of his mind when she placed a delicate hand on his knee. Their eyes met and a wave of tranquillity washed over the older man.

To the blonde, the Hispanic woman always seemed to have had a calming effect on him and he was grateful for that right now.

He was dangerously close to exploding and going on a killing spree before she stopped him, what good would that do besides terrify her more?

"Please, b-breathe and calm down."

Following her instructions, he did a slight breathing exercise to help extinguish to the inferno that was still raging on inside him. Meeting her gaze again, he smiled gently at her before slowly pulling her into a warm hug.

"Lia, I am so sorry. I want you to know, no harm will ever come to you, I swear on my life I will do everything I can to protect you. If you would let me, I would like to take this to Elias and ask him if I can investigate who this cretin actually is. I want you to be able to leave the castle's grounds without being fearful of him seeing you. I want for your love of figure skating to no longer be tainted with his looming threats. Just say the word and I will dedicate my life to finding him, but only if you would like me to."

Ophelia's chocolate orbs widened as she listened to the words that flowed out of the Irishman's lips and she felt her cheeks warm.

Never in her life did she think that she would have met a man that was as considerate and kind as this man she was currently wrapped around.

Reluctantly, she pulled away from Soleil's strong arms and looked up to stare into his beautiful grey eyes that she fell in love with. Before she gave him the answer he was waiting for, she took her time admiring his facial features.

The way long, golden lashes framed his eyes that held a mischievous glint within them, the perfectly flat brows that gave him this serious expression. His full peach coloured lips that she was desperately wanting to taste. The Irishman was gorgeous.

His ears were heavily pierced and she loved it. Both sides were adorned with a silver helix, industrial, faith, tragus, upper and lower lobe earrings.

She knew for a fact that he had gotten his tongue done around New Year's, as every time he spoke, she could see the glint of the metal ball.

As she continued to admire the adonis that sat before her, she heard him clear his throat and her eyes shot up to his.

Soleil's mouth was curved upward in a slight smirk and this set her face aflame as she realised he noticed that she checking him out.

As quickly as her gaze met his, they disconnected as she found her hands suddenly insanely interesting. Ophelia was mentally berating herself for making it so obvious that she was practically eye raping the blonde.

"Lia?"

"Y-yes?"

"You don't have to answer me right now, okay?"

Bright chocolate brown orbs met pale grey as she stared into the swirling depths. With her mind made up, she gave him a determined look and took a deep breath in.

"I want you to do it, Soleil."

16

"I want you to do it, Soleil."

Soleil slammed his fists into the tiled wall of his shower as the water rained down on him. Tears of frustration were spilling out of his eyes and down his pale cheeks, it had been almost a week (1) since he started his search for 'Alex'.

Even with all the resources and influence the Odin's Riders MC had, they were coming up short with barely any information.

It was infuriating the blonde man beyond his wildest dreams, he could not fathom how this man seemed to be essentially a ghost.

To him, it felt as with the lack of any progress in their search for Ophelia's ex-stalker, he was failing her and that if this continued she would never truly be freed from his perverse grasp.

Wiping his face clean of the mixture face wash, shampoo, tears and warm water, he quickly rinsed off the rest of his body. As he stepped out of the glass cubicle, his cellphone that was laying on his bed in his bedroom, started to ring.

Grabbing his towel, he swiftly wrapped the fluffy material around his lean waist and rushed into the joined room.

Practically diving for his mobile, he managed to hit the green answer button before the ringing could cease.

"Hello?"

"Soleil Walsh, get your Irish ass down to the King's office right now."

"But I jus-"

Before he could even finish his sentence, the line went dead and his friend hung up. Rolling his eyes, he tossed the cellular device back onto the plush comforter and made his way over to his large wooden wardrobe.

Slipping on a pair of dark grey boxer shorts, the blonde suddenly could feel a pair of eyes watching his turned back.

He made no movements that gave away that he knew that someone was looking at him.

Continuing, he slipped into a pair of light blue distressed jeans, a scarlet red shirt with the first few buttons undone and his signature leather jacket.

Kneeling, he reached for the shoebox that was under his bed, which held his favourite black combat boots.

Unknown to the person watching him, he also grabbed a small steel throwing knife and tucked it into his jacket sleeve.

After making sure the blade was secure, the Irishman calmly sat on his bed and discreetly surveyed his room as he pulled on his shoes.

He saw that his bedroom door was had been pushed slightly ajar, but it was such a tiny gap that one would not notice it immediately. Once he had finished tying the lacings, he walked out of the range of view of the small space.

Almost immediately as Soleil disappeared, he reappeared in the corridor, with one (1) of his pale hands wrapped around the young man's throat and the other held the knife just below his ribcage.

His grey eyes narrowed as he glared into the fearful green orbs and he tightened his grip on the peeper's neck. Hands clawed at his wrist's skin as the person desperately tried to replenish some of the oxygen that was rapidly depleting from his air supply.

"Who the fuck are you and why were you spying on me?"

The purple-haired boy tried to form words, but all that came out were strained gasps. Rolling his eyes, the Irishman relieved some of the pressure, however, he still kept his hand wrapped around his airway.

"I-I'm a n-new thrall a-and I was sent to e-escort y-you to the King's o-office, sir."

"If that's the truth, why the fuck were you looking into my bedroom. You would have fucking knocked and informed me of why you were here."

"Uh...I-I'm sorry, s-sir. P-please."

Something smelt fishy about his story and he quickly figured out that the young man was lying because there had not been any recent announcements about anything to do with prospecting members.

He decided that it would be best to check it out with his King.

Yanking the dyed hair, Soleil dragged him in the direction of Elias' office without saying another word. Along the way, the mysterious boy kept trying to free himself and constantly begged for the older man to let him go.

Ignoring his annoying pleas, his grey eyes narrowed into slits as the massive wooden mahogany doors came into view. He used his boot-clad foot to push the door open since his hands were a little preoccupied and strolled in.

Benjamin was the first (1st) to look up and was shocked by the sight that he was met with. Then Nova, Zia, Serah, Aster and finally the King, himself.

"Uhh, Leprechaun, why are you holding that boy by his hair?"

"None of you know this kid?"

All of the occupants in the room shook their heads as confused expressions spread across their features. The six (6) of them watched as the blonde's facial expression went from irritated to deadly and before any of them could react, he had slammed the young man into the wall.

"AH!"

Everyone but Soleil winced at the loud pained cry that was emitted from the boy's lips. They all wanted to try to stop him, but none of them had ever seen the normally jovial man with such a grave expression.

They were all in a state of shock and so they just watched as their friend dealt with the surprise guest. Unbeknownst to them, the blonde man had found himself in situations like this before because of his family's name and he had lost his temper at this point.

"Now, I am going to fucking ask you again. Who. the. fuck. are. you. It would be in your best fucking interest if you were to give me the fucking truth. Your life may depend on it. Choose your next words wisely."

Before his confession could spill out of his mouth, Ophelia and Reece busted through the large doorway. Letting out a scream, the Hispanic woman ran over to the Irishman and started to pull his hand off of the young boy.

Allowing himself to be gently tugged away, Soleil waited patiently as the two (2) Diaz siblings checked on the hunched over male as he gasped for breath. Once he had managed to regain his composure, identical chocolate brown orbs turned to the blonde.

"Hm?"

"WHAT DO YOU MEAN HM?!! YOU NEARLY STRANGLED HIM!"

The Irishman felt his left eye give a little twitch as he felt his temper flare at the accusing tone his friend was using. As if sensing that the younger man was working himself into a fragile state, Benjamin placed his hand on his shoulder.

Leaning down, he quietly whispered in his ear for only the other blonde to hear, "Breathe, you don't want to explode in front of Ophelia and cause her to become scared of you, as well now do we?"

Nodding, he followed the older man's advice and willed the storm that was brewing internally to calm and settle.

Opening his eyes, even though he did not remember closing them, the Irishman looked over to the short brunette woman who stood in front of him with concern etched into her features.

"Are you okay, Soleil?"

"Ja, sorry if I scared you just now, Lia."

Waving her small hand dismissively, her plump burgundy painted lips curved up into a small smile and patted his muscular chest.

"It's okay, you did not. Though, I have to ask, why were you trying to kill Kodiak?"

Kodiak is a name that is given to the baby boys in the English language. The meaning of the name is an island, and self-sufficient. The variation of transcriptions of the name includes Kodyak and a preferred name for boys.

"You know this kid?"

"Yes, we found out about him like fifteen (15) minutes ago."

The screams of confusion echoed throughout Elias' office as all its occupants except for the three (3) were waiting for the latter to elaborate further.

Reece sighed, he proceeded to give them a brief explanation about how Catalina and Dante had apparently hired the young Swedish boy to spy on the couple.

He had noticed the purple-haired young man earlier that day when he went to help his sister out in the kitchen.

Shortly after, he approached their parents and asked them if they knew anything about the person following their daughter.

Almost instantly, the married couple spilt the beans on their plans as they thought Soleil was in a relationship with their little girl.

"So instead of fucking asking her, THEY HIRE A POOR BOY TO FUCKING SPY ON US?!"

Brown curls bounced as the pair of siblings nodded their heads even though their faces held exasperated expressions.

They knew their parents were trying to show them they cared, but doing shit like that was just downright creepy.

The blonde man stooped in front of Kodiak, who flinched back on instinct. He gently placed a pale hand on his shoulder and apologised to the younger man. Turning his attention back to Ophelia and Reece, he responded,

"Get your parents in here, I need to have a word or two (2) with them, please."

A few minutes later, the older couple walked into the King's office, however, only Soleil and Kodiak were now residing in there. Motioning them to sit, the Irishman shot them an icy glare as they stared at him with a look of contempt.

"You two (2) better wipe those fucking haughty expressions off your faces. Don't fucking forget that I was the one who chose to look for you to get closure for your children. Now, care to fucking explain why you paid this poor child to spy on your daughter and me?"

Dante's thin lips curled into a sneer as he explained that they wanted to see why their precious offspring seemed so enamoured by him. He also expressed that he did not want the pair to mix as she came from a proud family.

"HAH! That's fucking rich coming from you, last I checked both of your offspring are old enough to make their own decisions on who they want to fucking be with. But that is not why I called for you both to be in here. Hiring a poor child to fucking spy on us. You two (2) may be new to the MC's life, but I'm sure you are intelligent enough to know that pulling a stunt like that is highly dangerous. This young lad could have been seen as a trespasser and could have been easily injured, or worse yet killed."

As the last words left the blonde man's lips, all of the blood was drained from Kodiak's face and he started to sob loudly.

Getting up from where he was currently seated, Soleil wrapped his arms around the crying boy and rubbed his back in a comforting manner.

"The story you gave him to tell if he were to be caught would have worked in any other club, however, the Odin's Riders MC has something special about them. We are one (1) big happy family and we announce everything to all of our members, we do not keep any of them out of the dark on anything, especially newcomers. You fucking endangered this orphan's life because of what? Idiotcity? Pride? I don't fucking know or care. He could have died today if Ophelia did not stop me or if I was another member. I am a trained killer and you knew that, but yet you continued out with this fucking dumbass plan of yours."

Turning his grey eyes away from the shell shocked couple, he gingerly picked up the now weeping boy and carried him out of the large office.

Nodding to Zia, the blonde man did not look back as his Herre entered to escort the Diaz parents to their rooms.

He took Kodiak to where Benjamin and Elias were waiting as they were going to offer him a chance to prospect for the club.

If he chose to, Reece and Reid were going to legally adopt him as their own child, allowing him to finally have a loving family.

As he left the dining room, his cellphone began to ring and the caller ID flashed with Aster's name. Answering the call, he listened as the young woman informed him that they had found a small glimpse of 'Alex' on security footage outside a small cafe where Ophelia was seen.

She informed him that she had already sent out a bunch of the club's members to find him and so far there was nothing.

However, the young woman told him not to lose hope as there was still a lot of ground to cover and they were not coming back until they got something.

"How did you know I was losing confidence?"

"My little sunshine, I have my doctorate in clinical psychology. I can hear the tells in your voice as you spoke to me and the desperation to hear some good news."

"Sometimes you're creepy, you know that?"

"Whatever, I enjoy it."

"Yeah, yeah. Just keep me up to date okay?"

"Of course, I'll let you go now. Tata!"

Once the call ended Soleil rolled his eyes and muttered something along the lines of, "Fucking weirdo." He decided since there was nothing that needed his immediate attention right now, he would go back and see how the little orphan kid was doing.

Plus, he felt absolutely wretched about what went down and wanted to make it up to him, since it was not Kodiak's fault.

Thinking about what transpired earlier had his fists clenching tightly to the point his rings were starting to dig into his flesh.

He was so excited to be able to meet the people that had raised one (1) of his closest friends, but also the person that held his heart even though she had no idea. However, now, he wished he never asked Cillian to risk his life for those filthy people.

The immediate differences between the parents and their children were so prominent that it was hard to deny.

Catalina and Dante were not what anyone in the castle had expected them to be when they had arrived, they were polite, now, disgusting.

It was as if having the knowledge of being with their children again and that there was no longer a looming threat anymore had set a switch off in them.

Shaking his head to rid his mind of those thoughts, he allowed a smile to spread across his face as he walked back into the dining room.

At that point, Benjamin and Elias had left, replaced by the couple who wanted to adopt the young boy. The sight that had greeted him was something he would never forget.

Kodiak had the biggest, genuine grin taking up his entire face as he was told about Reece's plans.

"Is it okay if I come in?"

Three (3) pairs of eyes snapped to face him and before Soleil knew it, Reid was dragging him further into the large room.

He found himself seated next to the purple-haired child, who surprised him with a hug, which he returned.

"I just wanted to come and say sorry to the little dude again. I can see he's very happy with the idea that you guys are going to become his new parents!"

"YEAH! I GET TO HAVE TWO (2) DADS! TWO (2)!!!"

Kodiak's excitement had the trio (3) of adults chuckling at how adorable he was and the fact that he was practically vibrating in his seat.

"I have an idea, hey kid! Do you want to go ask your Aunty Lia if she could make you something to eat?"

"YES YES!"

As the quartet slid out of their chairs and made their way over to the door, the adults were shocked when the youngest asked the Irishman if he and Ophelia were in love. He surprised them again with asking if he could be their ring bearer.

Choking on his saliva, the blonde robotically turned around to face the beaming child with a strained smirk as he slowly explained that the pair were in fact not an item. This made Kodiak rather sad as he mumbled that they looked at one another as his dads' did to each other.

Placing his pale hands on the small of the kid's back, the Irishman ushered him out of the room and in the direction of the kitchen. The group's mouths started to water as the delectable aromas that swarmed their senses.

Ophelia was standing at one (1) of the many large industrial stoves that the castle's kitchen contained. Her full attention was zoned in on whatever she was stirring and had not noticed the newcomers.

The sound of someone's phone ringing broke all of the culinary staff out of their musings and seven (7) or more heads popped up to look in the direction of the noise.

Soleil smiled sheepishly and waved his free hand in apologies as he backed out of the room.

"Soleil speaking."

"Hey, its Arin. We have the prisoner locked in a cell in the sub-basement. What do you want us to do with him?"

"One (1) question, why the fuck are you talking as if you read too many knight novels? To answer your own though, leave him there. I'm coming now, just prepare my special toys for me."

"Fuck you and no problem, where do you want them?"

"In the cell on the table, like normal and please make sure you have the hose this time."

"Got it."

A sinister grin spread across the Irishman's face as he thought about how long it had been since the last time he had gotten to play with someone. The Odin's Riders MC had a lot of enemies, but oftentimes, they tended to stay hidden like cowards.

The blonde found them to be a bore and that they lacked the necessary balls to call themselves rivals. Finally, however, he got a new doll to play with and release his frustrations on.

To the surprise of many, underneath his caring disposition, laid a sadistic monster.

Fortunately, he only ever unleashed his forbidden tendencies when dealing with someone that posed a threat to the club or had hurt someone he loved. Which was not often, leaving him to find new ways to occupy his ever-moving mind.

Clapping his hands eagerly, he reminded people of an excited child who was getting to open their birthday presents early. Walking passed the other members who were lingering in the foyer, he could not keep his grin suppressed.

As he walked out the front door, he remembered that it had been a while since he had gone to visit his best friend in the infirmary with everything going on.

Staring at the medical building, he made a mental note to visit him the following day before his last lesson with Ophelia.

By the time he had broken out of thoughts, he had found himself in front of the door that leads to the sub-basement. He could have used the one (1) inside the castle, but it was so much farther.

Warning Graphic Content. You have been warned

Nodding at the four (4) thralls that were standing out front on guard duty, he thanked them for opening the door.

Jogging down the concrete stairs, his combat boots making a loud noise as he moved, he completed the authentication process that was needed to enter.

Immediately his nose scrunched up in disgust as he smelled the rancid stench of rotting flesh and that reminded him to tell Benjamin that they needed to clear some cells. Covering his airway with the sleeve of his jacket, he walked further in and pushed open the door to his private room.

The sight that greeted him was a glorious one (1). His prey was bound, gagged and shirtless, allowing all to see his disgusting fat rolls. Turning to the chair that sat behind the large glass pane, he tossed his leather jacket to keep it safe.

"Låt oss börja."

('Låt oss börja,' translated from Swedish to English is, 'Let's start.')

Arin pulled out a manila folder and flipped to the page that he knew his friend was referring to with his statement.

Nodding his head over to Theo, who had positioned himself behind the chained man, he ripped the blindfold off of his face as well as the gag.

"Irwin Hindley, at the time of his crimes, he was fifty-one (51) years old and now is fifty-eight (58). He is currently unemployed with no family that speaks to him. The last job he had was a janitor at a restaurant until he was fired for harassing the female patrons. He used the pseudonym, Alex, as it was his deceased mother's first name."

The disgusting excuse of a man had the audacity to put on a brave front as he stared directly at Soleil and he coiled his lips back into a nasty sneer.

This did nothing but make the younger man burst out laughing, so hard that he had to lean against the wall for support.

"Old man, you should fix your face because you look fucking ridiculous right now! HAHAHA!!"

Irwin's courageous facade dropped instantly as he saw that his expressions did nothing but amuse his captor. Instead, it was replaced with a mixture of emotions that were mainly dominated by fear and anger swirled underneath.

"W-what do you want with me?"

"What do I want with you? Hah!"

Soleil moved forward and got right up in the older man's sweaty face. A threatening look entered his grey orbs and he uttered, "Why, I am going to make you scream."

He watched with a satisfied expression as the pale blue eyes widened with shock as his words sunk into his mind. Irwin was about to ask why was he doing this, but before he could, the Irishman slammed his elbow into the man's jaw.

The painfully loud crack resonated throughout the entire sub-basement and even through the closed doors, screams could be heard ringing out from every cell that contained a living person.

Ophelia's stalker's jaw had been broken and now he would not be able to spew bullshit without feeling large amounts of pain.

The blonde man smiled cheerfully before he stood upright and made his way over to the table where his toys were sitting.

Carefully, his eyes scanned over the metal surface before they lit up and he hurriedly pulled on some gloves along with a mask. Beneath the facial covering, he was grinning wildly as he heard his two (2) friends gasp.

"You guys can go wait behind the glass if you would like to watch."

Nodding, they did as suggested and took their seats as if they were in a hospital, viewing in on surgical procedure.

Waving the silver medical bone saw in front of his doll's gaze, he let out a loud giggle as the front of the pervert's pants darkened with his bodily fluids.

"Don't worry, this is only going to hurt a fucking lot. Theo, be a fucking dear and a tighten the chains so that he's more splayed out for me."

"Of course."

Once his request was completed, Soleil got to work. He slowly used the serrated blade to cut thin slivers of Irwin's skin off and allowed them to plop onto the floor.

Wails of pain left the older man's mouth as he was being butchered like a piece of meat.

After shaving off about fifteen (15) bits of his flesh, the blonde man made his way back over to his tools and set the metal piece down.

He shoved a capped needle into his front jean's pocket for later, grabbing a pair of tongs and walked back over, where he removed the man's khakis and boxers.

Using said pinchers, he roughly picked up the pathetic organ that sat in between his sweaty legs and snarled.

"You better not fucking piss on me or I will make your already torturous death even more painful."

Pulling the syringe out of his pocket, the Irishman bit the cap off and shoved the long needle down into his urethra. He left that there for now as he went on to use crimping pliers to crush his fingers and to rip off his nipples.

Blood splattered everywhere and the blonde rolled his eyes as he watched the pig's eyes roll back into his head as he fainted.

Letting out a loud tsk, his gloved hands dropped the forceps and cracked a vial of smelling salts under his nose, waking him up.

"Can't have you falling asleep on me now? The fun has just begun."

For the next five (5) hours, Soleil made small incisions all over his body, broken several bones, gouged his left eye and continuously shoved items up his rectum just as he said he wanted to do to Ophelia when she was only fifteen (15) years old.

"Now for the grand finale."

Snapping his gloved fingers in front of Irvin's badly beaten face, he directed his attention down to the needle that was still embedded in his penis.

"Wanna know that that is? I'm going to tell you anyway. This is fluoroantimonic acid, it is known as the world's strongest superacid is fluoroantimonic acid, $HSbF_6$. It is formed by mixing hydrogen fluoride (HF) and antimony pentafluoride (SbF_5). It is said to be the most corrosive acid known to man."

"SOLEIL ARE YOU CRAZY?!"

"Arin, you're acting as if you have not seen me do way worse."

A loud 'Hmph!' was heard, but he chose to not acknowledge his sulking friend as he knew what he was actually doing.

Whenever the Irishman was able to have his fun, Arin would try to do or say something to distract him, but it never worked.

Focusing back on the matter at hand, he watched as Irwin shook his head in a pathetic attempt to plea for him not to do this.

Chuckling, Soleil slowly pushed the pump down on the syringe, injecting the dangerous liquid into his victim's body.

Standing back, he watched as the aceite burned and melted away the flesh that was once his privates. His dying scream reminded the three (3) men of a banshee's wail filled with only agony and then it was over.

"Fucking finally, Ophelia is free. That was fun though!"

"Theo, get the hose."

"W-WHY DOES HE NEED THE HOSE?!"

"You need to be washed off before you leave, leprechaun. So stand still with your arms and legs apart."

"AHHH! COLDDDDD!!!!!!!"

17

"**F**ucking finally, Ophelia is free. That was fun though!"

"Theo, get the hose."

"W-WHY DOES HE NEED THE HOSE?!"

"You need to be washed off before you leave, leprechaun. So stand still with your arms and legs apart."

"AHHH! COLDDDDD!!!!!!!"

Turning the doorknob, Soleil pushed open the white wooden door and stuck his head into the hospital room. Quinn waved excitedly at his best friend from where he was sitting upright on his bed.

Entering the room, he made his way over to the plastic chair where he had often found himself sitting in when they had no clue when the ginger was going to wake up. The younger of the pair patted the older man's hand and gave it a squeeze.

"I just want to say that I'm sorry for now coming to visit you again. Things have just gotten so much more hectic with Dinah's wedding drawing closer, the lessons and also the Diaz's coming back."

"Hey, hey. It's okay, I understand, I heard about everything from when Benjamin visited and had brought the twins to meet me."

"Those two (2) are the chubbiest little things ever, I swear."

"They really are, but sunshine I have a feeling you did not come to talk to me about Jasper and Harper."

Allowing his head to drop forward onto the soft mattress, the blonde let out a loud but muffled groan. He heard chuckling come out of his friend and that made him slowly raise his head to show him that he was pouting.

"C'mon, you look adorable, yes but don't try to distract me, mister."

"Fine, fine."

He finally conceded, launching into a detailed explanation about everything that had happened yesterday with Catalina and Dante.

To be honest, he felt as if he had just added another problem to Ophelia and Reece's already mile-long list.

Soleil had honestly thought that it would have been a good idea to try to hunt down the parents and get some answers for their kids.

The last thing he had expected was that they were alive and well, but also some of the most repulsive people he has ever had the displeasure of meeting.

Considering how wonderful and just down to earth their children were, he had hoped that was where they had gotten that from. Apparently not. The eight (8) years that Reece had raised his baby sister had done them some good, it looked like.

The blonde also broke the news to him that Kodiak was going to be adopted by the mentioned and Reid.

He was so happy for the young boy, but he could not also help but feel guilty for nearly injuring him because of the sickening couple.

"Sunshine, I honestly hope that Odin never allows me to meet those two (2), I think I'd end up throwing a plate at them or something. People like that are just, I don't even have the words to describe them. I can't believe that the pair of angels came from those devils."

The last sentence had sent the Irishman into a fit of giggles that had left him gasping for breath in the most dramatic fashion. Quinn just shook his head and rolled his eyes at the scene that was playing out in front of him.

"Okay, okay, I think I'm good now. That's not all that happened yesterday, however."

"I know."

"HOW DO YOU ALWAYS KNOW I AM NOT DONE!?"

"Soleil, I've known you all my life. If I could not realise something as simple as this, what kind of best friend would I be?"

Waving a pale hand, it was the blonde's turn to make a motion of annoyance and he sneered jokingly at the ginger.

After that, he received a not so light slap on the top of his head and was basically ordered to finish his story.

He went on to recount the events that had taken place in the late evening to the early night with Irwin. The details had been dubbed down slightly for the sake of his friend's squeamish nature, but he refused to meet the hazel eyes that were staring at his bent head.

Quinn stared at the lowered head and deeply sighed, he knew that deep down that his best friend hated how much pleasure he derived from hurting others. Though, he often refused to admit it and more often than not, would attempt to brush it off with nonchalance.

Raising his arm, being mindful of the wires that lead to the machines he was still hooked up to, he tenderly rubbed the blonde's head.

The ginger had opened his mouth to say something, when he noticed streaks of water were running down his arms.

It took him a few seconds to realise that it was tears and that Soleil was crying silently. This caused the older man's heart to break as he realised that not only the guilt of being a sadist was weighing on his conscious, but also all the stress of the recent events.

"Sunshine.....c'mon, look at me."

He watched as grey tear filled orbs emerged from where they were hiding. When a broken hearted sob bubbled out of the younger man's throat, Quinn spurred into action.

Ignoring the throbbing in his back because of his quick movement, he pulled the Irishman into a hug.

Soleil's smaller body was shaking violently at the severity of his cries as he swiftly broke down and let out all of his frustration in his friend's arms. The comforting embrace that he was wrapped in made him feel safe as well as.

They stayed in that position for about fifteen (15) minutes before the blonde pulled away and quietly thanked the ginger. Shifting off of the bed, he gingerly sat down in his chair and waited for his companion to say something.

"I know you actually hate the way you are sometimes, Sunshine, even when you refuse to admit it. However, that does not mean you should not beat yourself up so badly about it, considering you rarely release that side of yourself. You said it yourself over a decade (10) ago, if someone were to hurt the ones you loved, you would have no problem inacting your revenge, but you would never do that to an innocent person. Therefore, don't do this and listen to your younger self's wisdom, okay?"

"You're right, of course, you're right. I guess with everything going on with Ophelia, I feel terrible for the way I am, Quinny."

"Dummy, I'm sure she would understand. She does not peg me as the type to be judgemental."

Nodding, the pair continued to chat for another hour (1) or so before it was time for the Irishman to leave and meet his 'special someone' as Quinn put it for his final lesson. Waving goodbye, he closed the door and made his way out of the club's infirmary.

After heading back into the castle to quickly shower and change clothing, Soleil met the Diaz siblings at the skating rink.

Reece was dropping off his sister today instead of him, since he had informed them that he would be a little late as he was going to visit Quinn.

During the drive to the building, the blonde was weighing between two (2) options. The first (1st) being that he waited to tell the Hispanic woman by herself about what happened. The second (2nd) was that he broke the news to both of them.

The latter seemed to be the better choice between the pair as he deserved to know as much as she did. So, that is how he found himself sitting the siblings down in one of the booths that were used for eating and telling them that he needed to discuss something with them.

"Lia, you know how you asked me to find the 'Alex' person?"

"Y-yes?"

"Well, yesterday, some of them members were able to track him down and apprehended him, bringing him back to the club. They took him to the sub-basement and I personally dealt with him, I promise you, Lia, that he will never hurt you again."

Reece and Ophelia's chocolate brown eyes widened in shock as his words settled into their minds. Soon after, he was bombarded with multiple questions on what was his actual identity and where was he now?

Raising one (1) of his pale hands to get them to be quiet, Soleil explained to them everything that he had found out yesterday from the file that Aster had composed. He informed them that if either of them wanted to see it, to just go ask her.

"To answer your other question, he is currently roasting, if you will."

"What do you mean, dude?"

"His body has been placed into the incinerator that's in the basement."

"W-WHAT?"

"HUH? WE HAVE AN INCINERATOR?"

Chuckling, the blonde knew it was a serious discussion that was taking place but their reaction was priceless. He forgot that they were not members of the club, but more so the culinary staff and friends of the Riders, meaning they did not know a lot of the compound itself.

"Yes, we do. It's to get rid of bodies from the sub-basement or if we were to be attacked, any corpses from the enemy would go there. Then their ashes would be thrown out."

"S-so, he's dead?"

"Yeah, Lia, I could not allow him to continue to live, so I killed him."

He braced himself for her to turn paler than a white sheet, but he got the opposite of the reaction that he had expected.

Her shoulders sagged in relief and her face finally lost the haunted look it always carried.

Sliding out from where she was seated next to her brother in the booth, Ophelia walked over to her saviour and pulled him into a hug.

She refused to cry as she did not want anymore tears to be shed because of that man.

Burying her face into his neck, she whispered a heartfelt, "Thank you for everything." It made him happy to know that she was not scared of him and that he was able to set her free from the demons that hid in her nightmares.

The trio discussed the matter for a few more minutes before they decided that they needed to get started or else they would not have enough time to finish.

Reece bid them farewell and reminded his friend to drive safely with his sister in the car.

Rolling his grey orbs, he chose to ignore what the Hispanic male said and chose to avert his attention to lacing up his skates.

Once they were on, the pair skated out onto the middle of the rink and Ophelia explained that the last move she would teach him would be the toe loop.

She got into position and started to walk him through what she was doing, so that he would be able to replicate.

"Begin by skating on a right back outside edge, with the skating knee deeply bent. Clockwise jumpers should start on a left back outside edge, and should reverse or mirror the rest of these directions, okay?"

"Got it!"

"Extend your arms into what is called the 'launch position.' The left arm should be straight in front of you; the right arm should be extended at the 'five o'clock' (5:00) position. Both palms should face downward."

Her body would gracefully flow into the steps as she spoke and anytime he asked if she could repeat, she would. The brunette's cheeks warmed as she noticed how intensely he was staring at her as to make sure he did not miss anything.

"Reach back with your left leg; extend it and point the toe down. Plant the toe pick firmly in the ice, preferably just to the right of the arc of travel of your other blade. Be sure to reach back; you don't want to trip yourself. Now, do not try to make yourself rotate, as it tends to cause an error known as a '"toe waltz.' The rotation will come naturally. Do imagine using your left leg like a pole vault, alright?"

A couple (2) of minutes later and they were on the last and final step for the 'toe loop.'

"Land on the right foot, on a back outside edge. As you land, extend your arms fully to the sides in normal skating position. Your right knee should be bent and your left leg extended strongly. Arch your back, keep good skating posture, and try to remain on the back outside edge. Then smile!"

Soleil felt as if his heart was about to fly out of his chest and into the hands of it's rightful owner that stood in front of him. The smile that had spread across her face, brought several butterflies to his stomach.

To him, she looked absolutely breathtaking and he so badly wished he could take her into his arms.

However, he knew not to do that because it could possibly freak her out and even though they were much closer than they were before, it did not mean he'd cross her boundries.

She then repeated the steps a couple (2) more times just to make sure he had gotten the hang of it and now it was his turn to see if he could land it.

Just like all the other times that they had practised advanced moves, his hands started to feel clammy and his mouth went dry.

The last thing he wanted was to accidentally hurt himself or worse, injure Ophelia in the process in the case, he were to spin out of control.

As if she could read his mind, the brunette slid over to him and placed her dainty hands on his shoulders.

"You're gonna be okay, I know you will. You've been a natural on the ice since we got your balance in check, so please do not start to doubt yourself now. The fear that runs inside of you will not carry you to success, but will drag you down to the depths of failure. So, cm'on, believe in yourself like you do for me."

Once her words settled in, they dissolved all the frantic thoughts that were running rampant inside of his mind.

Grinning widely, the Irishman nodded and slid into the first (1st) position and waited for the countdown from his teacher.

"Get ready......Set......Start!"

The beautiful melody flowed through the building's sound system as he started the routine that would lead to him completing the 'toe loop.'

Taking a deep breath in, confidence took over and his pale limbs moved gracefully through the air.

At the climax of the music, his figure skates left the ice and his body rotated into a full three hundred and sixty degree (360) revolution in the air.

Then his right foot landed back onto to the slippery surface and then he slid into the finishing pose.

Immediate applause was heard off to his side and as he opened his eyes, that he didn't realise he had shut, Ophelia was cheering loudly for him. She was practically leaping in excitement and had a proud look shining on her face.

"YOU DID IT! SEE!"

"I FUCKING DID IT! HOLY SHIT!!!"

The rest of the class was spent with the pair celebrating and going over the old moves so that they were perfect on the day of Dinah's wedding. Now they were walking towards the blonde's Audi, when he suddenly stopped.

Looking back at her friend, the Hispanic woman asked him if something was wrong and the words that left his perfect lips nearly had her jaw dropping to the floor.

"Lia, would you do me the honour of being my plus one (1) to the wedding?"

"Uhhh....why not!"

18

"Lia, would you do me the honour of being my plus one (1) to the wedding?"

"Uhhh....why not!"

A serious conversation was destined to happen on this day between the Diaz siblings about what they were going to do with their parents.

Reid was also going to join them as they had many times, unknowingly harassed him for being with their son.

It was a topic that no longer could be pushed aside for another day and they needed to figure out how to reign it in.

The trio (3) could foresee that a nasty storm was brewing and they did not put it past the older couple to start disrespecting the club's high ranking members.

So, that was why they were found sitting inside of Reid's bedroom with the door locked as if they were a bunch of children attempting to hide from their parents. Resting on the bed, in the middle of them was a notepad, along with a set of pens.

They had been sitting in mind-numbing silence for the past half an hour (30) and they had yet to come up with any kind of solution.

It was beginning to drive all of them absolutely insane as they found it should not have been this hard to deal with this.

Many persons would think that they should have gone to Elias or someone who was in charge, but they were tired of having everyone solve their problems for them. It was time for them to resolve something on their own.

However, they were unaware of the fact that Serah had been watching them earlier in the day and noted it to her husband about what they were up to.

Their King was then informed and he passed out the order, that unless they asked for help, leave them to do it on their own.

This caused several members to protest, but they were quickly silenced by the raise of his hand as he told them to think about how they felt.

It was obvious that they appreciated all the assistance that they had received in the past, but that had nothing to do with it.

"You have to remember that they even though they are not trained like we all are, they are not incapable of resolving humane issues. So, do as I say and don't interfere unless they express the need for aid."

Back in the waiter's bedroom, crumpled balls of yellow lined paper littered the carpeted floor as tensions grew. Ophelia's head was being held in her hands as she let out a small scream, she could not believe how hard this was to do.

Her brother was no different, only that he was cuddling into his boyfriend's shoulder and muffling his cries of irritation there. Reid was unconsciously rubbing the older man's back as he was deep in thought.

Suddenly a knock on the door sounded and broke the rigid atmosphere that resided inside the chambers. Sliding herself off of the mattress, the brunette walked over to the door and pulled it open.

Her chocolate brown eyes widened to the size of saucers as she saw Catalina and Dante on the other side. Raising a perfectly curved eyebrow, she asked them, "What do you want?"

"We've bought a house, so you and your brother need to go pack."

This statement caused Reece to fly up from his place in between his partner's legs and to his younger sister's side.

His gaze hardened as he looked at the two (2) people he had to, unfortunately, call his parents.

"The fuck do you mean that we have to pack?"

"Reece Eduardo Gabriel Diaz, that is no way to speak to your parents!"

"Save me that shit, Catalina. You are not the mother and father that I grew up knowing, so I will fucking speak to you, however, I please."

The acid that spewed out of their son's mouth had stunned the older pair as their mouths fell open and their eyes rapidly blinked.

Crossing his arms, the young male gave them a bored expression as he impatiently waited for them to break out of their stupor.

Reid stayed back as he knew this was something that needed to happen, though something inside of his gut told him that he should call for backup.

From the short time that the couple had taken up residence in the club's castle, he knew that they liked to cause a ruckus.

Grabbing his cellphone from the nightstand, the Swedish man dialled Soleil's number and prayed to Odin that he would pick up. It seemed like the Gods were on their side today as the blonde picked up on the second (2nd) ring.

"Hey, Reece's Big Cup!"

"Hey, Sol. We need your help, the Diaz parents are here, they're demanding that Ophelia and Reece leave with them as they bought a new house. Please, come quickly. You know how they can get and I have a bad feeling about this."

"I'm on my way."

Once those four (4) words travelled through the receiver, the line went dead so he hung up and hoped that things would not escalate before he got there. The Irishman could feel the veins in his neck pulse as his anger grew.

Waving Zia and Astrid over, he explained to them the situation as he walked. Both women agreed to help and expressed that they had been waiting for the longest time to put those two (2) ungrateful bitches in their places.

Along the way, they passed Nova, who they told to call her husband and let him know what was going down. She nodded and did as she was told, watching as they continued moving quickly without breaking stride.

Spotting the quartet (4) that had moved out into the hallway, Reid's bedroom door was shut as if it was an act put forth to make sure he was spared of anything that may conspire.

The blonde's grey eyes narrowed as he rushed forward and he slid in front of Ophelia, just as Dante's hand slammed down to collide with his cheek.

His head snapped to the left and the noise his neck made was enough to have the woman he protected screaming. It sounded as if the bone itself had been snapped with the force of the hit he had received.

Everyone watched in shock as his pale body fell lifelessly to the wooden floor. Shoving all of them out of the way, Astrid carefully lifted his head onto her lap as she checked to see if her friend was okay.

"He's alright, though where his ring slammed into his temple knocked him out. I don't know if it has caused any internal injuries, we would need to take him over to the hospital for Luke to look at him."

"Blix, take him and I'll deal with our little trouble makers."

"Right."

No one made a move to stop the Asian woman from effortlessly picking up the taller man and walking away without looking back.

Once she was gone, Zia made her move and within the blink of an eye, the elder couple had a pair of guns pressed against the back of their heads.

The Russian smirked slightly and explained to them that it would be best for them to leave or else they may not be so lucky again.

Catalina and Dante were granted the ability to stay alive if they were to work with the Puerto Rican Mafia.

Eight (8) years later, they were saved and their debts were cleared by the newest Don, finally being allowed to see their children once more.

However, all they had done in the short time they had been back was cause pain and suffering to everyone around them.

"I will give you two (2) options. You either leave this place and never try to contact any one of us again, or you die. What will it be?"

The Diaz siblings gasped as they heard the words that were being spoken to their parents and neither of them had any idea what to do. Ophelia was torn, but deep down she knew that Zia spoke the truth.

Nothing would put an end to this unless they were given an ultimatum and now it was up to the adults to make their final decision.

Though the looks on their faces spoke volumes on how they were feeling about the threats to their life once more.

Catalina turned to her son and daughter, begging them with her eyes to assist them. Reece felt as his eyebrow twitched and he spoke up before his sibling could.

"If you think about asking us to save you, you're fucking delusional. First (1st) of all your fucking husband tried to slap my baby sister and then ended up injuring my close friend. Secondly (2nd), both of you have only tried to order us around since we have become reacquainted, acting as if we are not grown-ups ourselves."

He watched as the elders' faces turned grave and rage seemed to have taken over as Dante lunged forward to beat his eldest child for such insolence.

Before he could get within range of the young man, the bedroom door beside them was flung open.

To everyone's surprise, Reid ran out and hopped on top of the threat, detaining him with a level of skill that only one (1) of them knew he possessed. For extra measure, the Swedish man slammed his captive's face harder into the flooring.

"Do not. Ever. Try. To. Lay. Your. Filthy. Hands. On. What. Is. Mine."

The growl that had left his partner's mouth, had Reece's cheeks being dusted by a dark pink glow. Shaking his brown curls, he mentally reminded himself that now was most definitely not the time to be getting turned on right now.

Although, it was quite hard when you have a man as good looking as his, who literally threw himself into the fray to protect him.

Then, as if someone threw a bucket of cold water on him, he remembered that Soleil tried to do the same thing and he got hurt.

At that moment, Elias came walking down the hallway at a brisk pace and the look on his face was enough to out someone six (6) feet under, several times. Ignoring the bumbling Hispanic parents, he stood in front of their children and looked down at them.

"Make a decision right now. Do you want them to live or to die?"

"HUH?!"

"WHA-?!"

"You heard me. As you can tell, they're quite hellbent on the two (2) of you going with them and controlling your lives. So, what will you do?"

Ophelia thought about what her employer said and she realised that he was correct. Even if they were to leave peacefully, which was obvious was not going to happen, they would more than likely come back to try to retaliate.

No matter how amicable she wanted her relationship with her parents to be, it was crystal clear that there was not a chance they would uphold that idea. She had made up her mind, although it was not an easy one to make.

Reece seemed to be on the same wavelength as his younger sister, they already did not accept the fact that he was a gay man. He knew that they also did not welcome the idea that their daughter may be in love with a biker.

At the end of the day, their children's happiness was the last thing they cared about as obviously shown by their previous actions.

The brunette could not overlook it and how his so-called father could carelessly attack his own. His final decision had been settled.

The siblings looked at one another and simply nodded. No words needed to be spoken for one another to know that they were thinking the same thing.

Turning to face the person that had acted as guardian for them, even though he was younger than one (1) of them, they informed him of their decision.

Smirking, he acknowledged them with a slight nod of his head and he ordered Zia to do what needed to be done. A maniacal grin grew on the normally stoic Russian's face as she asked the young waiter to help her drag the pair to the sub-basement.

"Is she going to torture them?"

"No, however, it's best that no one hears the gunshots and you don't need to see it. Would you like for them to have a funeral?"

"Hmm....No. You can just bury them, they relinquished their rights to be our parents a very long time ago."

Ophelia's statement had the two (2) older men gaping at her with their mouths open. They never thought the day would come where she would be absolute on a decision, without the need to apologise.

That just showed them how much she had grown as a person since joining the club and meeting a certain blonde Irishman. Speak of the devil, Elias' phone started to ring and the screen flashed showing that it was Luke calling.

"Hey Doc, what's up?"

"You and the Diaz siblings should come to the infirmary."

"Is something wrong?"

"Yes, he's thrashing around, trying to get out of the damn bed to go look for his woman. If he keeps this up, he'll aggravate his injuries like the idiot he is."

"We're on our way."

Hanging up, he turned to the other two (2), who was staring at him with worried expressions and he had to explain to them what the call was about as they walked.

Once she heard what he was doing, Ophelia rolled her eyes and started to rant about how he was a dummy.

As amusing as it was to see the young woman so worked up over the man she had feelings for, they needed her to calm down before she whipped out a chancla to beat him. By the time they approached the glass sliding doors, her temper had died out.

Now that anger had been replaced with distress as she wondered how badly her 'father' had hit the older man.

Before their feet could hit the ground, Doctor Luke was standing in front of them, pulling them along.

With the pace, he had been yanking them, they arrived at the Irishman's room in record time and they could hear him clearly now as he yelled to be released.

Reece muttered that he was making so much noise, you could practically hear him when you were in the elevator.

Pushing the door open, the woman he had been fighting all of the nurses to find, walked right into the room, perfectly unscathed.

This caused him to stop being restless and he allowed the medical staff to adjust anything that was pulled out of place.

Luke walked in with the other men in tow as he beelined for his patient and started to check up on his injuries. Deeming him fine, he immediately started to berate the young man for being so stupid and risking hurting himself more.

A rather hilarious argument broke out between the two (2), with one (1) throwing very childish and odd insults at the other. It seemed that the exuberant blonde was doing just fine and so Elias decided that he would take his leave now.

Bidding the siblings farewell, he walked out and informed his wife that their friend was perfectly okay.

Inside the room, Luke told the siblings that he suffered a minor concussion, along with a dislocated shoulder from when he fell to the wooden floor.

Profusely apologising to the hospitalised man, who waved it off and told them that he would do it again if he had to.

Ophelia then started explaining what happened after he had gotten hit and the things that had to be done.

She also remarked Reid's incredible martial arts skills that they never knew about. It was truly an impressive sight, to say the least, and Reece piped up, just to gloat about how hot his boyfriend was.

Rolling his pale grey orbs into the back of his head, Soleil threw out a retort that he thought that statement was in fact true. Chuckling as he saw his friend's face turn bright red as his jealously and possessive nature exploded out of him.

"WHAT DID YOU SAY!"

"That your little waiter boy is indeed eye candy."

"C'MERE YOU LITTLE SHIT!"

"Awwww, Reece's Pieces are you getting a little jealous?"

"STOPPPP, YOU TWO (2)!!!!!"

19

"WHAT DID YOU SAY!"

"That your little waiter boy is indeed eye candy."

"C'MERE YOU LITTLE SHIT!"

"Awwww, Reece's Pieces are you getting a little jealous?"

"STOPPPP, YOU TWO (2)!!!!!"

Doctor Luke had just signed the release forms for Soleil, who had sped out of the hospital as soon as he was done.

The older man was sure the dark blue ink had not even fully dried yet as he shook his head and headed back into his office.

Now that a week had passed, he was free to do whatever he wanted once more as both of his injuries had fully healed.

Just in time too, as the day after tomorrow was Dinah and Cillian's wedding, so he definitely needed to be discharged.

Most of the Odin's Riders members had seen a flash of blonde hair zoom past them as they were patrolling the grounds or going about other duties.

That was how fast he was moving as he rushed to get back into the castle so he could give Ophelia the dress that he had bought for her.

Zooming past everyone, he threw his bedroom door open and dived under the bed. Grabbing the small black box with a lavender ribbon tied around it, he placed it on the bed and opened his wardrobe.

He took out a white garment bag that held the gown and went back to his mattress to pick up the other gift he had for the siblings.

Making his way down to the floor where her room was located, he used his boot-clad foot to knock on the wooden surface.

Ophelia opened it and smiled cheerfully when she saw that it was the Irishman. Then, she remembered that he had just been discharged so he was pulled into the room and sat on her single bed.

"How are you feeling and what's with all the stuff?"

"I'm fine, stop worrying that pretty little head of yours. This is for you, but you can't open it until the day after tomorrow."

"Okayyy, thank you. You are the sweetest."

Taking ahold of the hanger, she went over and hung the mysterious garment on her closet's door. Strolling back over to the Irishman, she watched as he picked up the box and grabbed her much smaller hand in his large one.

"C'mon, we have got to go get Reece, who's in the kitchen from what Serah just told me."

Allowing herself to be tugged along, the brunette was having a hard time keeping up with the brisk pace the taller man was using.

Willing her short legs to move quicker, she was practically running behind him at this point.

Soon enough the torture was over and she thanked the Gods that her arm had not been yanked off. To be honest, she was genuinely surprised to see that her legs had not been worn down to stumps.

Soleil's pale grey eyes zoned in on his friend, who was heavily making out with his boyfriend against the marble counter.

Making pretend gagging noises, he turned to face Ophelia, whose face had turned a bright red when she finally saw the sight.

Clearing his throat, the blonde said, "Yo, get a fucking room! This is where we get our food created, c'mon guys! You're gonna make your baby sister's face melt off."

The speed in which the couple separated, one (1) would have sworn that a barrel of ice-cold water had been dumped on them. Reece slowly turned to face his sibling and at least had the decency to look embarrassed and apologetic.

Shaking her head, the young woman placed both of her hands on her face and tried to get rid of the sight so they don't haunt her forever.

Don't get her wrong, she was perfectly fine with him having a male partner, but them making out was not something she needed or wanted to see.

The three (3) men watched warily, wondering if she was going to drop to the floor in shock or something, suddenly, her shoulders started to shake.

At first (1st) they thought that she might have been crying until she threw her head back and she fell into a fit of giggles.

When the rest of the kitchen staff found the quartet (4), they were either laying on the floor or slumped against the fridge, dying from laughter.

No one knew what they were laughing at and it seemed neither did they.

Once everyone had calmed down and regained their composure, Ophelia reminded the Irishman that he had wanted to tell the pair something.

As if lightning had struck him, Soleil jumped up and picked up the box from where he dropped it.

"This is for...well just open it."

His grey orbs followed as Reece carefully untied the purple ribbon that was wrapped around the gift and pulled the top off.

His lips curved up into a lopsided smirk as the trio's eyes widened in shock and then squealing.

"ARE YOU FUCKING SERIOUS RIGHT NOW!?"

"OH, MY FUCK!"

"IF THIS IS A DREAM, NEVER WAKE ME UP!!!"

Chuckling, he explained to them that after everything that happened in recent events, he thought it would have been necessary to have something nice done for all of them.

The blonde also expressed in a way it was an apology for bringing those wretched people into the castle.

"It wasn't your fau-"

Raising his hand, he silenced the protest that was coming out of his friend's mouth.

"I know it's not, but it feels as if too. I risked my sister's fiance/soon to be husband's life to save them, instead of fucking endangering my own. I thought that bringing them to see you two (2) would be the best idea I had ever had but fucking turns out that it was nothing short of a fucking failure. It ruined the good memories you had of your parents and they just brought you more pain. You guys got hurt instead of healing. I'm so sorry."

Ophelia ran from where she sat at the marble counter and rushed over to the object of her affection. Grabbing his pale face in her dainty hands, she forced him to look into her eyes and she shot him a small smile.

"Sol, you are not at fault and you should not feel bad at all, okay? Cillian chose to help us all by doing what he did and I'm sure that if he did not want to, he would not have done so. Please do not blame yourself, the only people to do so are dead now. You should not allow yourself to take on the responsibilities of those horrible pairs mistakes, please. It pains me to see you like this."

Running her thumbs under his eyes, she wiped away the tears that he did not even know he had shed. He softly thanked her and expressed how truly grateful he was to have her in his life.

The blonde went on further to state he did not know what his life would be like without her.

Pulling Soleil into a warm and affectionate hug, hoping that it showcased how she felt without the need for words.

Shortly after, the pair separated and sat back down on the cushioned stools to talk about the present.

"Dude, I can't believe that you managed to get all four (4) of us a bloody reservation in Sapphire Light! That restaurant is super hard to get into and I heard that they have a three (3) years waiting list as of right now. So, how did you do it!?"

"I know the owner actually. His sister is an old childhood friend of mine and we are still pretty close, even though I have not seen her in a few years, so I called her to ask if there was a chance we could have a private table for just us. She was the one (1) who technically got us in."

On the outside, Ophelia was smiling, but internally she could not help but feel a rather large twinge of jealously course through her veins.

She knew that he had said they were just childhood friends, but who knew what could happen if they were to see one another in person.

Unfortunately for the brunette, her mind refused to stop the upsetting thoughts that were running rampant inside of her mind. Frowning slightly, she quickly stood up and made her way over to the refrigerator.

Sticking her head inside, she welcomed the cool air that brushed across her face and pretended to look around for a drink. Grabbing an apple cherry juice bottle, she closed the door and plastered a bright fake smile on her face.

Immediately, the Irishman noticed something was off about her, but he decided that he would ask her about it in private.

For the next few minutes, the quartet (4) discussed what to wear and if all of them were going to just take one (1) car.

Once they were done, the couple left to go start to get ready and before Ophelia could leave, the blonde gently grabbed her wrist.

"What's up?"

"I should be asking you that."

"What do you mean?"

"After I started talking about Minerva, your whole body language changed and when you came back from getting your drink, you smiled. However, it was not your regular one and then I realised it was the one (1) that you gave to your parents."

"N-no, nothing is wrong."

"Lia, I know you. I've seen your genuine smiles and that was not it, c'mon talk to me. Maybe I could help."

Sighing, the Hispanic woman averted her gaze from the taller man's face as she mumbled that she might have been feeling slightly jealous.

Placing a large hand on her small shoulder, Soleil shook his head and inwardly smirked.

"So that's what that was all about. Before you go digging yourself into a further hole in your subconscious, Minerva is happily married to her girlfriend of seven (7) years. She and I have never been romantically involved and we always thought of each other as family. Don't worry your pretty head about it."

Making his way over to the only woman he ever felt so strongly about, he wrapped his arms around her. He whispered that they should go get ready before they run late and unwrapped himself from around her.

Heading to his room, he unlocked the door and walked in, beelining for the bathroom to rush through getting ready.

Stripping out of his clothes, pale hands ran over his side where the large intricate leviathan tattoo laid.

Smiling, he shook his head and jumped into the shower. Carefully, he lathered up his hands with cedarwood and sage scented shower gel.

Once he was finished cleansing himself, he washed off the soap suds and grabbed a towel, wrapping it around his waist.

Throwing open his closet doors and stared, trying to think about what he wanted to wear. Since Sapphire City was a pretty upscale place, so he decided that he was going to go with an indigo dress shirt and black pants.

Reece and Reid were sitting downstairs wearing similar outfits to their friend, though the Hispanic male had a dark grey suit jacket on as well. Ophelia exited the elevator at the same time as Soleil and they nearly crashed right into one another.

"Wow, you look absolutely incredible."

The blonde's grey orbs raked up and down her body taking in her outfit. She was wearing a pastel purple corset vest with a pair of lavender slacks and nude pumps.

Her neck was adorned with a silver chain and a diamond pendant with matching studs in her ears.

She styled her loose brown curls in a low ponytail that sat at the nape of her neck with a few strands flowing in front of her face.

Her makeup was kept minimal with a little eyeliner, mascara and clear lip gloss.

The Irishman clenched his fists to stop himself from pulling her into his arms and ravaging her on the spot. Shooting her a lopsided smirk, he extended his hand out to her and his grin widened as she slipped hers into his.

Leading her to where the couple was waiting, they stood up and greeted them, before walking out to the blonde's car.

On the drive to the diner, Reid told several jokes that he heard when he was growing up in the country side of Sweden that had all of them dying.

Pulling into the private parking spot that he had gotten reserved for the night, Soleil parked the car and opened his date's door for her. Praying silently to the heavens that she would not trip over her pants legs, the brunette took his hand.

Once she was fully out of the car and standing on the concrete, Ophelia did a small happy dance with her upper body.

Chuckling at his little sister's ridiculous antics, Reece snuggled himself further into his lover's arms.

Soon they were all seated inside of one of the three (1/3) private booths that sat on the indoor balcony.

Soleil and Reid sat next to one another while the Diaz siblings took the other side, so that their dates were across from each other.

While looking over their menus, trying to figure out what they were going to order for their appetizers, a gorgeous tall Taiwanese woman sauntered up to their table. Immediately, the Hispanic woman stiffened and her dark brown eyes narrowed.

Before the rest of the occupants could ask her if she needed something, Soleil jumped out of his seat and pulled her into his arms.

"Evangeline! Tá sé chomh maith tú a fheiceáil!"

"Sol! Tá sé chomh fada sin!"

('Evangeline! Tá sé chomh maith tú a fheiceáil!'='Evangeline! It's so good to see you!')

('Sol! Tá sé chomh fada sin!'='Sol! It's been so long!')

"It really has been. Oh! How rude of me. Angel, these are my friends."

Inwardly, the Irishman winced as he desperately wanted to call a certain brunette, who was wearing the sexiest outfit he had ever seen, more than a friend. However, he still was on the fence about how she truly felt about him.

"Hello, it's wonderful to meet you all!"

Returning, what she hoped was a pleasant smile, the Hispanic woman tried her best to compel her temper from flaring out. She knew why she was jealous, but at the same time, she knew she had no claim on the gorgeous blonde.

"This is Reid, his boyfriend, Reece and Ophelia, who is this idiot's younger sister. Guys, this is Evangelina, Minerva's wife."

After introductions were over, the Irish woman bid them a pleasant evening and told them that if they needed absolutely anything, they could always call for her. The rest of the night went amazingly and all four (4) of them had a wonderful time.

"Dude, fucking thank you for this. We needed it!"

"That is a true statement, right there, babe."

"Really, thank you, Sol. It was the best surprise ever."

20

"Dude, fucking thank you for this. We needed it!"

"That is a true statement, right there, babe."

"Really, thank you, Sol. It was the best surprise ever."

The Day Before Dinah and Cillian's Wedding

"SOLEIL WALSH! GET YOUR FAT ASS UP RIGHT NOW BEFORE YOU'RE LATE FOR YOUR FUCKING FLIGHT!"

The blonde man flew out of his bed, completely disoriented, with only his pastel yellow pyjama pants on and his hair sticking up in several different directions.

Spinning around, he looked for the person who had just screamed at him.

Hearing an attempted covering of a snicker, he spun to face the doorway and as that Elias and Benjamin were standing in the opening of the portal.

Standing up straight, pale grey orbs narrowed at the sight of his two (2) friends, who were grinning widely.

In the blink of an eye, the three (3) men were on the ground, with the older pair landing flat on their backs with the youngest on top of them. Soleil slapped their shoulders lightly and then got off of the both of them.

"Why are you crackheads waking me up?"

"Um, because Ophelia has been downstairs for the past thirty-five (35) minutes, waiting on you to get your ass to her."

"Huh? Why?"

"You are hopeless. What is tomorrow?"

"Uh, Thursday?"

Rolling his bright blue eyes at the pathetic attempts that the Irishman was making to remember what was the following day, Benjamin knocked on the latter's head.

"Yep, hollow, Ellie."

"I knew it, Benji. Sunshine, it's your sister's wedding day tomorrow and today you are supposed to fly to Greece so you can be there on time."

The pair watched as the blonde's face drained completely of blood as he let out a loud screech and flew into his bathroom. Shaking their heads, the King and Herre left their friend to hurry himself up.

Fifteen (15) minutes later, Soleil was fully packed and dressed, running through the castle's main hallway on the ground floor to reach the car.

Reid was the one (1) driving the pair to the club's private airfield and he knew that meant he had to hurry up.

He practically threw himself into the open SUV's door and slammed it shut, exhaling out loudly as he made it. Giggles emitted from the driver and passenger seat, which caused the blonde's head to snap up.

Joining them on their journey was Lyra as she had never been that far out of the city, so she asked Elias if she could tag along to sightsee.

After greeting everyone in the car for the first (1st) time that morning, they were off to the land of olives, Greece.

The Wedding Day

Ophelia had found herself waking up an hour (1) before they were actually supposed to start getting ready. She looked over at the bed that was resting parallel to hers, only to see a small tuft of blonde strands peeking out of the top and toes at the bottom.

Her roommate had practically cocooned himself in the blanket and became a rather large lump on top of the mattress.

Covering her mouth with her hands, she tried desperately not to awe out loud, as she had never seen the older man like that before.

Soleil was deep in sleep and cuddling his other pillow as if it was a teddy bear that he never wanted to let go of. The brunette did not know if she should try and snap a photo of the cute moment that had been presented to her or just leave him be.

After deeply contemplating the idea, she decided that it was worth a shot trying to capture the sight. Quietly, she slid out from under her pine green fleece blanket and grabbed her phone off of the wooden nightstand.

Retracing her steps, she sat on her knees on her soft cushion and took a few pictures from that angle, then moved around for a few more.

Just as she finished taking her tenth (10th) image, the comforter mass started to shift as the Irishman started to wake up.

Scrambling away from his side of the room, Ophelia acted as if she had just been checking her phone the entire time.

Grey eyes popped open as the blonde rolled over onto his back and he scanned the room.

Instantly, he knew she was up to something as she kept shooting nervous looks his way and it took a little bit for his lethargic brain to figure it out. The moment he did, he gasped and flung himself out of bed.

"Lia, did you take pictures of me while I was asleep?"

"Uh..no..what on earth would give you that idea? Haha.."

"Oh, nevermind, I don't know either."

Turning around, Soleil pretended to start to walk away and waited until he heard the quiet exhale that breezed past her lips. Suddenly, he turned around and grabbed her cellphone from her hands.

Booking it, he beelined for the bathroom and shut the door behind him, making sure to turn the lock. The Hispanic woman started to bang on the door, albeit not loudly as she was not trying to be impolite and wake up everyone else.

Smirking, the grey-eyed man turned his attention to the unlocked device in his hands. She had not been able to exit her camera app when he had woken up and therefore he saw all of the photographs she had taken of him.

He was about to make a move to unlock the door when a text message notification caught his attention. It was from Reece, which left an unsettling feeling in the pit of his stomach. Opening the chat, he realised that she had sent him the pictures of him slumbering.

The thing that made it worse was that his friend replied saying that he forwarded it to Elias, Nova, Benjamin, Serah, Zia, Ivan, Astrid, Lennox,

Arin and Quinn. Groaning out loud, he quickly sent a text to the current deadman walking.

It read, 'I am going to shoot you in the kneecaps when your sister and I get back."

Flinging open the door, the blonde stalked over to Ophelia and handed her phone back to her without a word. Reading what he had texted back to her brother, she shook her head when she saw what he did.

"Honestly, he deserves that. I sent it to him cause he sleeps the same way and most definitely not to send to everyone we're close with. If he runs, I'll trip him, don't worry."

"I know you didn't mean for that to happen. I'm not mad, it's not like I don't have embarrassing pictures of all of you."

"What?"

"Nothing. Anyways, we have about fifteen (15) minutes before everyone else gets up. Should we go get something to eat and start to get ready?"

"Sure, let's go."

After Soleil threw on a shirt and the brunette threw on a jacket, the pair silently exited their room. Walking through his childhood vacation home, he pointed random things out to Ophelia and softly told her the tales of that particular item or spot.

Once they made it to the kitchen, the Irishman offered to make food, telling her that she was basically on vacation. That meant no work for her. He whipped up some giant bacon cheddar bagels and two (2) cups of fresh pomegranate juice.

Soon, they were both back in their shared room and being the gentleman that he was, the Irishman offered for her to use the shower first (1st). While she was getting clean, he took the liberty of pulling out her garment bag and shoes from the closet.

Shortly after, the brunette woman emerged from the steamy bathroom, her short-form was being swallowed by an ivory fluffy robe.

Averting his eyes away from the tantalizing view that she was presenting, the Irishman stood from where he sat and rushed into the joint room.

A grin found it's way onto Ophelia's face at the display of respect she had just witnessed and shook her head. It wasn't that she did not appreciate the sentiment, however, she couldn't help but want for him to fulfil her naughty desires.

The thought of him just acting out some of the dreams she has been having recently, made her face glow bright red.

Quickly shaking her to dispel the dirty images that were flying passed her closed eyelids, she dusted off her robe and went over to the vanity that sat in the corner of the room.

By the time Soleil had finished taking a shower and shaving his face, his date had finished her makeup, along with her hairdo. Turning to face the older male, she squeaked and once again found herself blushing at the view.

The light ash blonde locks were dripping wet and she watched, completely mesmerised, as he brought a pale hand to push the strands out of his eyes.

His toned abs were on display along with the large leviathan tattoo on his side, with water running down his chiselled body.

Unknowingly, her brown orbs started to follow a droplet as it slid down his torso past his v-line and under the beige towel that was secured lowly around his hips.

She did not notice that he had been calling out to her for the past couple of minutes until he suddenly appeared in front of her.

"Lia? You look quite flushed, are you feeling alright?"

She desperately wanted to create some space between the two (2) of them, unfortunately for her, behind her was a concrete wall. All the young woman could do was nod without so much as a peep out of her.

Furrowing his brows, the Irishman didn't believe and thought that maybe she was starting to feel ill because she was nervous to meet his family. Although, he could not blame her as the Walsh Clan were a very intense bunch.

"You sure? If you're nervous about meeting my folks, it's alright."

"It's n-not that."

"Then, what is it? Lia, I just want to help."

At this point, the brunette could not hide it any longer, as the last thing she wanted was to make Soleil feel bad.

Swallowing her nerves, she took a breath in to muster up the courage to tell him the truth.

Just as she was about to tell him, her guardian angel arrived in the form of his dad, Haru, who had burst through the door. The loud noise of the wood meeting the wall cause the pair to jump apart.

"Dadaí, cad atá á dhéanamh agat?"

"Tháinig mé chun beirt a sheiceáil ort, cén fáth a bhfuil tú nocht?"

"Níl mé nocht!"

"Níl tú gléasta freisin."

('Dadaí, cad atá á dhéanamh agat?'='Dad, what are you doing?')

('Tháinig mé chun beirt a sheiceáil ort, cén fáth a bhfuil tú nocht?'= 'I came to check on you two, why are you naked?')

('Níl mé nocht!'=' I'm not naked!')

('Níl tú gléasta freisin.='You are also not dressed.')

Rolling his grey eyes, he repeated his initial question towards one (1) of his parents, with both of his hands on his hips.

Haru explained that he was just coming to see if they were awake and if they had already had breakfast, which he realised they had.

"Well, get out."

"Rude, you wound me."

"Out."

Waving goodbye, the Japanese man left the bedroom and made sure to close the door behind him. Making his way over to his side of the room, the blonde locked the entrance as he walked passed it.

Soleil quickly slipped on a pair of black boxers under the towel and once he did that, he let it drop to the floor. On the opposite side of the space, Ophelia's body was on fire and she felt a sensation she never felt before.

Her core was starting to become wet and she just knew if she stood up, her juices would start to run down her legs. Cursing inwardly, she started to fill her mind up with images of all kinds of disgusting things to calm down.

Once, she felt as if she could get up without falling down on wobbly legs, she stood up and walked over to where the Irishman had kindly placed her garment down.

Silently, she thanked her past self for putting on her panties and bra under the robe, when she had gotten out of the shower.

Dragging the metal zipper down, the Hispanic woman nearly dropped the gown as more of it got revealed.

Removing the plastic covering, she let out an audible gasp, the cerulean coloured floor-length wrap dress had a thigh-high slit on the left side and it was gorgeous.

The long sleeves were slightly loose and had shimmering champagne lace accents running along the entirety of the dress. Opening the shoe box, she smiled as there was a pair of matching blue ankle strap wedged heels.

Once she had finished dressing, Ophelia added some finishing touches before she walked over to the floor-length mirror to finally take a look at the completed outfit.

Dainty hands flew up to cover her mouth as she gasped at the person she saw before her on the reflective surface.

The slight noise she made was enough for the blonde man to look up from where he was seated, buttoning up his dress shirt. His grey eyes went wide and his jaw slammed to the floor as he took in the sight that she presented.

"Sol, are you alright? Do I look bad or something?"

Her second (2nd) question seemed to snap him right out of his stupor and before she knew it, the taller man was directly in front of her with his hands on her shoulders.

"Fuck no. You look irresistible, I'm not going to lie, but I genuinely think Dinah is going to have some competition for best dressed at her wedding later today."

"Oh my! Soleil Walsh, do not say that! You're incorrigible."

Chuckling, he shook his blonde locks and went back to his side to finish getting dressed without adding another stupid statement. Once the Irishman was finished, he fixed his mulberry coloured tie and grabbed Ophelia's hand to leave the room.

His suit was completely black except for said tie as he told Cillian that there was no fucking way he was going to put on a steel grey suit. Then he proceeded to curse the older man out when he asked if he would wear a white shirt.

It wasn't that he was opposed to the colour white, but being around his family in that shade was not the smartest idea.

Especially when the already rowdy clan got enough alcohol in their system to kill at least five hundred (500) people.

The Wedding Ceremony

The soon to be married couple were currently exchanging their vows and during that time Soleil couldn't help but admire his older sister.

She was always someone he had looked up to and now seeing her looking like a goddess, while her face wore a shit-eating grin as she married the love of her life.

When her electric blue eyes met his pale grey ones, the younger of the pair sent her a cheeky wink as a way to let her know he was happy for her.

Shortly after, he watched in slight horror as the newlyweds locked lips in a passionate kiss as they were now legally bounded forever.

"I need to bleach my eyes now. You guys need to get a room or stop eating each other's faces, there are children here! Have some shame!"

"SOLEIL, LEAVE YOUR SISTER ALONE!"

"I'M GOOD, ATHAIR!"

"Why you-"

21

"SOLEIL, LEAVE YOUR SISTER ALONE!"

"I'M GOOD, ATHAIR!"

"Why you-"

Haru and Auberon were sitting on their private family jet, across from their son, who was doing his absolute best to avoid their gazes.

The young Hispanic woman who was seated next to the latter was fast asleep with headphones on so she could rest in peace.

The quartet (4) were currently on their way back to Sweden after spending the last nine (9) days in Greece on a small family vacation.

The last few days were a breeze, but that could also be attributed to the fact Soleil had actively been avoiding his fathers.

Now that they were all confined to the rather large but still constricting area, with no room escape, he had resorted to just not looking at them. In most persons eyes, it could be deemed a childish move, but he did not care.

The younger blonde knew that if he even so much as acknowledged his parents, even just the slightest could prove to be fatal. There were so many unanswered questions that were swimming in mismatched eyes.

"Son."

"Soleil."

"MY DARLING CHILD!"

Wincing at the high decibels that his overdramatic Athair had yelled, he rolled his grey orbs into his head and sighed.

There was no way he could pretend like he had not heard them now, thanks to the living, breathing foghorn.

"What do you want? Besides to blow out my eardrums and make me deaf before my fucking seventy's (70s)."

SMACK!

"Ow! What was that for?"

"That was for answering your father in such a rude manner, just because you're twenty-four (24) doesn't mean you can be disrespectful. He was calling you because he is worried, that's all."

The cold-tone that accompanied a twin look from Haru had the Irishman regretting how he had answered his old man.

Deep down, he knew they meant well, but sometimes he felt like they still treated him as if he was a toddler, who could not be doing anything for himself.

Sighing, he met the mismatched eyes that belonged to Auberon, which were swimming with copious amounts of disbelief and hurt. Soleil had not meant to hurt the older man's feelings.

"I'm sorry, Athair. What was it you wanted to ask me?"

"It's alright, I know I can be a handful sometimes, but we were just wondering how everything was going between you and her?"

The ash-blonde followed his father's finger to where he was pointing at a slumbering Ophelia and unknowingly, the corners of his lips quirked up in a fond smile.

Turning his attention back to the older couple, he motioned for them to get up and follow him.

The trio (3) moved to the back of the plane so that they were out of earshot if the brunette was to wake up, but not completely out of sight that she could possibly freak out.

The Japanese man nudged his son with his elbow and told him to hurry up.

He started by telling them everything that had occurred in the recent events before the wedding and tried to catch them up to date as fast as possible.

When it came to telling them about what he had done to the disgusting man, he briefly hesitated as he knew it was not something his parents liked to hear about.

As if sensing that his son needed a boost of courage and comfort, Haru pulled Soleil into a tight hug.

Quietly, he told the younger male that he figured that he wanted to tell them something that had to do with the darker parts of his job and that it was alright to go ahead.

That made his heart swell with love as he knew that even though they were quite apprehensive about him joining the club at first (1st), they loved to hear about his day.

He appreciated that they put up with hearing about what he liked to deem his 'dirty little secret.'

Swallowing the rather large lump in his throat, the Irishman slowly walked his dads through everything that had taken place a little while ago.

Although, he did leave out the most graphic parts because even though they wanted to hear about it, that did not necessarily mean they wanted to be scared.

He finished the recap with a small amount of comic relief, telling them about how he had to be hosed down like a damn dog.

That had sent the two (2) older men into raucous laughter, but they were quickly dialled it down when they remembered Ophelia was still asleep.

Taking a peek over the seats in the rows in front of him, Soleil checked to make sure they had not woken up the poor girl. She was extremely tired from all of the festivities as she obviously was not used to it.

Blowing out a massive breath, he slid back down into his seat and gave them the all-clear. As if lightning had struck him, the Irishman jumped a couple (2) of feet in the air because he remembered something that had happened just yesterday.

"Why the hell did you just fly out of your seat as if it was burning hot like the fires of hell?"

"Dadaí! You're so mean to me! Anyways, I just recalled something I overheard Delphine tell Lia before we left."

"Ohkayyy...?"

"Honey, you're going to have to give him a bit of a bigger nudge. Your Dad is a bit slo- OW!"

Haru had punched his husband in his arm, which caused the older man to let out a yelp like a puppy who had fallen over.

Pouting, Auberon looked up at his lover with watery eyes cause he was a big baby and this caused the former to feel quite bad for hitting him.

Leaning over the armrests, the Japanese man gave him a chaste kiss on the lips and murmured an apology before he retreated back to his side. Soleil silently gagged and pretended to shield his eyes from their public display of love.

"You guys are disgusting, seriously."

"Shut up. Go on with your story."

"Well, it happened right after the two (2) of you had gone to check on things with the pilot, I was making my way over to Lia, to help her with her suitcases, since she bought a bunch of stuff for Reece and Reid. But, when I got closer, I heard Delphine ask her when was our wedding going to be. I cannot recall the last time I had ever felt so embarrassed and walked away so quickly."

At some point, during the mortifying story, he had averted his eyes away from his parental figures and instead of the laughter he was expecting, his heavily pierced ears were met with absolute silence.

Deciding that it would not hurt to look up and attempt to gauge their reactions from both of their faces. The sight that greeted him was nothing short of comical, Auberon's dual coloured eyes were wide with shock and his lips were mimicking the movement of a fish's mouth.

The priceless response, however, came from Haru, who's normally stoic face was coloured a bright red and his tattooed hands were clutching the material of his sweater, right where his heart was located.

It looked as if he was in the midst of going into cardiac arrest and to be very honest, Soleil did not know if it was okay to laugh or if he should be worried.

Deciding to attempt to snap them out of whatever trance the couple was in, he started clapping his hands in front of their faces.

"I'm just going to go back over by Lia and nap the rest of the flight. Both of you just don't die in this state."

Shaking his head, the blonde stood up and quietly eased into his seat next to Ophelia, who unsurprisingly was still dead asleep. He laid his head back onto the cushioned armrest and allowed his eyes to flutter closed.

Five (5) Hours Later

Ophelia had just waltzed into the castle's kitchen to grab something to drink when she felt a large hand grab her by her shoulder. Before she could scream, a familiar Swedish accent yelped, "Wait!"

Whirling around, the young Hispanic woman placed her hands onto her hips and looked up to shoot Ivan with an icy hot glare.

She proceeded to scold the older man for practically shaving off a good chunk of years off her lifespan.

Once she was done, all the noirette did was throw his head back and release a bellowing laugh as if he was not phased by her warnings.

She supposed with them being in the business that they were in, her hollow threats were quite easy to spot.

"Alright, what did you want before you nearly killed me?"

"Well, Solar System was support to have told you, but he's busy bawling his pretty little eyeballs out. I came to inform you that our Quinny boy has finally been cleared and released from the hospital by Doctor Luke."

Even though the words look like they had been heard by the brunette, her mind only honed in on the words, 'bawling', 'his eyes out' and 'released from the hospital.' Everything else had gone in one (1) side and out the other so fast.

Gripping Ivan's arm in a vice-like grip, she ordered him to take her to where the pair of best friends were and also inquired if the rest of the club had been notified.

Not even so much as flinching at her grasp, he nodded and explained to her that she was the last to know.

Seeing how her facial expression dropped and the hold on his forearm had loosened considerably. He quickly realised that he needed to rectify the situation before his friend got swallow by her thoughts and insecurities.

"What I meant was that Solar System had wanted to tell you, himself, but when he saw his best friend actually standing upright and walking around, the waterworks started. Remember, you are part of this club and our family. Ophelia, you mean a lot to all of us, probably the world to a certain blondie."

The last part was said was under the noirette's breath, who was praying the woman had not heard him, despite how close the pair were standing. It seemed as if luck was on his side, the brunette seemed oblivious to his murmuring.

"C'mon, let's go. They're all in the meeting hall. You know, since otherwise, not everyone would be able to fit and ontop that damn Leprechaun is probably having a fucking cow since we've been here for about ten (10) minutes."

Ophelia giggled but allowed herself to be practically pulled to their destination. When the pair finally arrived, all eyes were on them as the door had slammed shut quite loudly, but familiar pale greys were the ones (1s) she searched for.

Removing herself from her place by the door and Ivan, she made her way over to where her brother was seated. Which conveniently was right next to Soleil and Quinn, the latter, excitedly pulled her into a hug, giving her a tight squeeze.

Once she was released from the warm embrace, she was promptly seated between the two (2) men and told to pay attention to Elias now.

Following the ginger's gaze, she saw the power couples seated on the raised dais with a microphone in each hand.

The entire club paid watched as Benjamin stood up from his seat and walked over to the middle of the platform. He tapped on his mic and jokingly looked at it crosseyed to lighten the atmosphere of the room a bit more.

"Welcome, everyone again. I've gathered all of The Odin's Riders members here because as you can obviously tell, our beloved giant has been released from the hospital and of course, we are all over the fucking moon. We've all missed his bright smile and wonderful personality. So, before I hand the stage over to our wonderful King and my Ellie, I just wanted to say, WELCOME BACK QUINNY!!"

The massive room lit up with screams of happy greetings and applause, which caused the gentle giant to become flustered. He had always known he was loved by the club and its members, but now he knew really just how much.

Not long after, the hall quieted down and watched with great anticipation as their leader took his Herre's place at the front of the stage. His full lips were curved into a small smile as his emerald green eyes swept the room.

Raising the mic to his mouth, he also wished the redhead a warm welcome back and stated that he was extremely glad to see that he was healthy.

"Now, before the festivities and celebrations begin, there is one (1) thing I would like to address with you all. Last year, a horrible event took place and none of us was aware, except for the victims. Despite how close we all are, they were all scared out of their minds and refused to tell even their closest confidants. The fact that I, myself never even realised what the fuck was happening underneath my own castle and nose, I can never forgive myself. Quinn Fletcher was the one (1), who was the most deeply affected and my friend, I am so unbelievably sorry for not being able to stop your pain before it even began. Can you find it in your heart to not only forgive me but all of us here today?"

As the words left the tall brunette's lips, he lightly gestured for the Swedish man to come and join him where he stood, which he did. Once he arrived, the microphone was handed to him and he was told to say whatever it was that he wanted.

Tears had already welled up in his amber eyes as he watched every single one (1) of the members faces and saw how truly sorry they were.

However, when his eyes met Soleil's, that's what sent opened the gates to the dam of tears that he was holding back.

The amount of guilt, sorrow and underlying self-blame that were swirling in the depths of those grey orbs did something to him.

Maybe it was the fact that he knew that the blonde felt as if he was responsible for him trying to end his own life or the knowledge of how worried the latter had been for him since day one (1).

He did not know, what he did know was that not for a moment did he once blame any of these people in this room and he never would.

Quinn released a shaky breath and expressed all his feelings of gratitude and love for them, letting them know that he wasn't mad.

A few moments later, the entire club was mingling with cups filled with the ginger's favourite non-alcoholic drink and miniature plates with finger foods of his choice.

Soleil and Ophelia were chilling near the doors, watching as their friend threw his head back at a joke that Arin told him.

"He really looks as if he is having so much fun."

"That's true, but unfortunately, the hardest part is still not over."

"How right you are, Lia, but this time, he won't be going through it all on his own and will never again."

"You can definitely bank on it."

22

"He really looks as if he is having so much fun."

"That's true, but unfortunately, the hardest part is still not over."

"How right you are, Lia, but this time, he won't be going through it all on his own and will never again."

"You can definitely bank on it."

It had been a few days since the club's celebratory party about Quinn's hospital release and speedy recovery.

Now everything seemed to be basically right back to normal and they all fell into a routine of the Diaz siblings, Reid, Soleil and the former eating breakfast together in the garden.

Whenever the quintet (5) were together, there was relentless teasing about how much a certain Irishman liked the only female member of their small group. Fortunately, very fortunately for him, the playful jabs seemed to go right over her head.

Sometimes, though, the jokes became a little too obvious and she would nearly catch on, but then the topic would switch.

That did not mean that whenever she was not there because she had to be in the kitchen, that the teasing stopped.

It would be blasphemous to even harbour that idea.

The mornings that it was just the guys, Soleil would be at the end of every joke and his seemingly unrequited love would be the star of it. He knew that his friends meant well, but sometimes he did not want to think about how little chance he had.

Even though, there was too much evidence piling up that showcased that the Hispanic woman more than likely felt the same way as he did.

Reece knew better than anyone how he was feeling and tried his best to console him, along with some not so subtle reminders.

The entire club was baffled at how blind he could be as well as they were worried at how easy his mind would backtrack into a tunnel of insecurity.

After about a week (1) had passed, Quinn had gotten fed up with his best friend and decided it was time to pull out the big guns.

By big guns, he meant Lyra, Nova's mother. The woman was a goddess with giving advice and helping others realise how they were feeling about certain situations. Somehow, she always knew before the actual person, couple or group knew.

There was a running joke and bet that she was indeed psychic or at least had some sort of superpower with the way she knew basically everything.

No one would have batted an eyelash if one (1) day she came out and informed them that she was a witch or something.

The gentle giant had mulled over the idea of meddling for a few hours before finally making up his mind and making his way over to her salon.

His need for her help was not the only reason for his visit, albeit was his main, but he was in dire need of a haircut as well.

Pushing opening the clear glass door, his senses were immediately filled with the wonderful and pleasant smell of warm vanilla. Ducking through the doorframe, he let out a small curse when he still hit his head.

"Quinn! What brings you here, honey?"

The silvery voice of Lyra greeted him and the ginger could not help himself, he could feel his lips curve up into a large smile at the sight of the small woman.

Her sunset dyed hair was piled up on the top of her head in a mess of curls, but somehow it suited her.

He assumed she had just finished with a client as her clothes were still covered by her ocean blue apron and her disposable gloves were still on.

Quinn quickly explained to her that he was wondering if she had time to give him a haircut.

"Darling, you don't even have to ask that. Come on, let's get you situated in one (1) of the backwash units that way I can take a look at your locks and then immediately wash, okay?"

"That's fine with me."

A bright smile was sent his way and it warmed him from the inside out. She reminded him a lot of his adoptive mother, who was a short, petite woman, who was able to light up a room with her presence alone.

With a little extra pep in his step, the large man followed closely behind her and sat down into the plush leather seat.

His eyes fluttered close as the pleasant sensation rushed through his body as she ran her hands through his mane.

"Something's on your mind, isn't it?"

Prying open his eyes, Quinn tried to blink away the bleariness that appeared as he became more relaxed.

Looking up, he met the knowing gaze that was so eerily similar to Nova and Serah, maybe because they were all mothers now.

"Yeah, it's got nothing to do with me though, it's about Soleil."

The second the Irishman's name left his lips, her steel grey orbs widened and seemed to twinkle with a piece of unspoken knowledge. Giggling, the brunette brought her hands up to her face and smiled knowingly at him.

Lyra already knew where this conversation was probably headed, considering the blonde was his best friend and she had a similar conversation with Ophelia when she was trying to discover her feelings for the former.

However, something told her that it would not be the same problem, since there was no doubt in her mind that he was aware of how he felt.

She couldn't place her finger on it, so instead of trying to jump to conclusions, she opted to ask her client.

"What about that little ray of sunshine?"

"Well, I'm sure you're clued up with that fact that the idiot has a very obvious crush on Ophelia."

"I am, honey, even a blind man could see how much he's already fallen for that lovely girl and vice versa."

"True, except for him. Solar System seems to be going at a tug of war with his mind and emotions because one (1) minute he's pretty certain that she does like him, then the other is she doesn't. It's been really noticeable these past few days and I honestly have run out of things to tell him and reassure him that he's not even remotely wrong."

"I'm guessing you want my help and possibly want me to talk to him. Am I correct?"

The ginger nodded and sat back up, allowing her to towel dry her hair. He wondered if she could do it sometime today as he was afraid and honestly quite worried that if they waited any longer, he'd fall off the precipice in despair.

Lyra assured him that as soon as they were done here, she'd close up the salon for a few hours and go drag him away to talk.

If anyone deserved to be happy, it was those two (2), as after everything that Ophelia went through and everything that Soleil did for her was any testament.

Forty-five (45) minutes later, the appointment was finished and Nova's mother had cleaned up her workstation. After locking the doors to her work, she pocketed the keys and made her way through the compound towards the massive castle that sat in the very centre.

She had no idea where to look for the Irishman, so she decided to locate her daughter and ask her if she had any idea. Heading up to her shared office, she knocked on the door and was greeted by the deep baritone of Elias.

Pushing open one (1) of the large doors, she walked in and watched as he perked up with a large grin stretched across his face. She watched as he eased his large frame out from behind his desk and walked over to her.

Engulfing her into a tight hug, which she readily returned, Lyra reached up onto her tiptoes and ruffled his curls.

"Hey, Mama. What brings you here? I know we have dinner plans later tonight, but do you need to take a raincheck or something?"

"Hey, honeybuns that's not it. I came looking for my little star to ask her if she knew where Soleil is."

"Oh? Well, Karlek is upstairs taking a nap right now. However, if you want I can call him for you."

"That would be great, thank you."

Making his way back over to his wooden desk, Elias reached for his cellphone, before he paused and smirked evilly. He decided to then press the intercom button to announce it throughout the entire castle.

"Soleil Walsh, come to my office, now."

Said blonde heard this and he visibly blanched at the thought that he might have been in trouble for doing something.

What he had done, he did not know, but still knew better than to make his King wait.

Setting down the rifle that he had been cleaning, he quickly assembled it and placed it back into its protective casing.

Once that was finished, he left the secured armoury and rushed to the elevators.

Unfortunately for him, they were seemingly taking way too long for his liking and he abandoned the idea of using them.

Running up the stairs, he practically threw himself through the office doors and landed with a pained grunt as his dick collided with the floor.

"I don't know why you just flew through my doors like you were James Bond, which clearly now we know you would never be, jackass."

The Irishman stopped his pained rolling around on the floor for a brief moment to send a glare up at his friend. The pair waited until he was no longer dying on the floor and being a drama king.

Gesturing for him to take a seat next to Lyra, the large brunette quietly excused himself to give them some privacy.

Once the door was fully shut, Soleil turned to give the older woman his undivided attention.

"What did you need me for?"

"Well, don't get mad at your friend for this, but Quinn passed by the salon earlier for a haircut and I could tell that something was weighing heavily on his mind. I asked him about it and it turns out he was worried about you, still is too. He informed me about how you feel about Ophelia, though that is quite obvious, but especially about your recent insecurities. So, I'm here to talk to you about that, he wants to help you, but didn't know how else to."

Nodding, the blonde understood why his best friend had done what he had done and he appreciated that he reached out to someone who could offer assistance.

Although, he really had not expected anyone of them to realise that he was spiralling.

The longer he thought about it, the more that previous thought was the dumbest fucking thing that had ever crossed his mind in his twenty-four (24) years of life.

Shaking his head, he got up from his seat and offered his hand to the sunset haired woman.

She shot him a questioning look but still accepted the kind gesture. Chuckling, he explained that they could go get something to eat or drink while they talk to make it less formal. The pair got into the blonde's car and drove to a small café that was known for its scrumptious pastries.

Though, the entire of The Odin's Riders MC would argue that Ophelia's confections were the best in the entire world and absolutely nothing could compare.

But, considering they were going to be discussing the beloved head pâtissier, it would not be smart to go to her for food.

After the two (2) got their orders, which for the Irishman was a slice of strawberry shortcake and a cup of black coffee. The Swedish woman had gotten a cup of hibiscus tea and a chocolate chip muffin.

As they indulged in their treats, he explained to his lunch partner what was going on inside of his head and what exactly had seemed to have brought on those particular thoughts. It started after the incident with the Diaz parents that had sent him into the infirmary and had yet to leave.

It would always creep out of the dark recesses of his mind, like a little voice in the back of his brain saying that she did not want him or who would want a monster that derives pleasure from hurting others.

The narrative was always the same and the words would repeat in different ways or sometimes scenarios. Deep down Soleil knew that he was being completely irrational but at the same time, he could not help himself.

Once he was finished, Lyra took a sip of her drink before she rested her chin on her clasped hands and stared at him. The look in her grey eyes seemed to say she was thinking and reading him at the same time.

After a few minutes had passed, she leaned back in her seat and told him that he was being the biggest idiot. That had the young man sputtering and stumbling on his words as his brain short-circuited.

"W-what?!"

"You heard me."

"Yes, I did, but the question is why would you say that?"

Rolling her eyes in the same manner that he had seen Nova do plenty of times in the past few months, she released a loud sigh. He could practically see the exasperation rolling off of her in humongous waves.

"It's quite obvious to everyone how the two (2) of you feel about one another, however, it seems that you guys are the only ones who are dense to it."

"Wait. You're telling me that she likes me as well?"

"Is the sky fucking blue?"

"Uh, yeah."

"There, you have your answer. Now, c'mon go tell her."

"R-right!"

Soleil quickly threw down enough money to cover their food and drinks, along with a little extra for the waitress who had served them. Once that was taken care of, the pair flew out of their cushioned seats and into his car, speeding back to the club.

On the drive back, he had asked Lyra to text Reece to let him know what he was going to do and somehow pry his sister away from the kitchen.

He got back a confirmation that all of that was already taken care of and she was waiting by his bedroom.

Thanking the brunette woman for talking to him and helping him come to a massive realisation, he waved her goodbye.

Heading into the castle, the Irishman beelined for the stairs and ran all the way up to the floor where his bedroom was located.

As he rounded the corner, he saw a familiar figure wearing a pastel pink cardigan over a white tank top and a pair of ivory loose-fitted linen pants. He opted to whistle out to her then yell her name and disturb anyone else who were in their rooms.

Ophelia's head snapped up and their eyes met, if anyone else was there, they would say that the moment they saw one another, a spark erupted between them.

Waving shyly, she watched as the taller man made his way over to her and unlocked his door.

She giggled as he gestured for her to go in first and did a horrific British accent as he said, "After you, m'lady."

Now they were sitting side by side on the soft mattress, in silence and Soleil was silently cursing himself as this was not how he wanted this to go.

In his head, he had the words he wanted to say and how exactly he wanted to express himself, yet here they were.

He jumped when he felt a hand rest on his clenched fists, that he didn't even realise that he was doing this. Looking up, he was met with concern swirling in the chocolate brown orbs that the Irishman had grown to love.

"Are you okay, Sol?"

"Yeah, sorry. Fuck, this was not how I wanted this to go at all."

"Wanted what to go?"

This was it. This was the moment that he had been waiting on for the longest while that he could remember. Taking in a deep breath, he smiled gently at her and interlaced his fingers with her.

"Lia, I like you. I mean, I really fucking like you and I know I'm normally quite smooth, cause have you seen my dad. That's a joke, oh Odin, I'm butchering this. I've had feelings for you since the day we met, I don't know, the moment I saw you, my knees went weak and I couldn't think straight. You have this thing about you that makes everyone love you and ontop of that, you're the sweetest thing in the world besides your desserts. I guess, what I'm trying to say it, I like you a lot and fuck, I need to know how you feel about me, please."

Soleil held his breath and he could not bring himself to look at her because it would be too much for him to handle. The atmosphere was still, but not necessarily uncomfortable, it just seemed to be there with no presence of emotion.

"Sol, I feel the same way. When I first (1st) met you, I was terrified of everyone and would hardly speak to anyone. Then you came along and even though I was scared, you made me feel so safe and comfortable. Even when I shied away from everything, you still kept pushing, but at the same time stepped back when you felt like you needed to give me space. That's only the tip of the iceberg when it comes to how I feel about you and why I like you. To answer your question is, yes, I do, Soleil."

The blonde released the breath he was holding and he could see his vision was becoming blurry as tears welled up in his grey orbs.

Placing her hand under his chin, Ophelia got him to look at her and she graced him with a shy smile, as she started to cry as well.

With shaking hands, Soleil gently cupped her face and silently asked if he could kiss her, to which she nodded.

Leaning forwardly, their lips met in a soft and slow kiss, immediately, sparks were erupting through both of their bodies.

Soon, the two (2) of them parted for much-needed air and leaned their foreheads against one another. Both of them could not believe that this was something that had happened, yet it was also single-handedly the best thing ever.

"Wow."

"I know right."

"Can-Can we do it again?"

"Fucking duh, Lia."

23

"Wow."

"I know right."

"Can-Can we do it again?"

"Fucking duh, Lia."

The next few hours had been spent with the newly confessed love-birds making out and relaxing in bed, exploring one another's bodies.

Now it was dinner time and even though, they were technically 'a couple', they opted not to announce anything yet.

The reason behind this decision was that Soleil wanted to ask her properly and then they could go about telling their family. Now, it was once again a nervous moment for him to work up the nerve to ask her out on a date.

He knew he was being ridiculous considering she confessed her feelings for him and everything that took place after that was a massive testament to it.

It was still nerve-wracking, the last time he could remember doing something like this was probably when he was seventeen (17) years old.

It feels even scarier than it did eight (8) years ago and he had a feeling it was because of how strongly he felt for the woman who was pressed up against him right now.

The blonde knew he loved her and that he hoped this could go on forever, so why not make the start now.

"Babydoll?"

"Mm?"

"Would you do me the honour of allowing me to take you out on a date in a couple (2) of days?"

He chuckled as he watched her head fly up to meet his gaze and see the amount of excitement that was spreading across her face.

"YES! OH MY GOD YES!"

"Haha, awesome."

After a quick peck on the lips, the pair settled back under the covers and continued watching the tv-show that was currently playing.

The Day Of Soleil and Ophelia's Date.

It turned out to be a very hectic day for the club's kitchen staff as one of their thralls requested a bunch of baked goods for his daughter's birthday party. This meant that Ophelia was up to her elbows in dough, sugar and icing.

Had it not been for the rest of the workers, she would have started to panic that she would not have enough time to go get ready for her date. Thankfully, he told her to be ready for quarter to eight (7:45 PM) and to get somewhat formal.

She had already called and booked a hair appointment with Lyra to do her hair at six o'clock (6:00 PM).

Astrid and Zia were meeting her there so that she could just get herself ready there, instead of having to go all the way back to the castle to her bedroom.

Time flew by relatively fast and before she could blink, her shift was over. Reece helped disrobe from her chef's smock and watched as his little sister flew past everyone to the front door.

He watched and made sure she was out of his line of sight, before whipping out his phone to text Reid.

('Hottie' is Reid and 'My Baby' is Reece)

My Baby: Target has left the rendezvous.

Hottie: Baby, you're not a real spy. Anyways, we're on our way to the place.

My Baby: You're no fun, babe.

Hottie: Yeah, yeah. Go start on your part of the plan.

My Baby: Fine, I'm going now, love you.

Hottie: Good boy, love you too.

Over at the hair salon, it was bustling, no one sat still besides Ophelia, who was ordered to not move as the head stylist trimmed the ends of her long curls.

Through the large mirror, she saw as her friends rushed around with different garments overflowing from their hands.

It kind of reminded her when the entire club was freaking about executing Serah and Benjamin's babies' first (1st) birthday party perfectly.

The thought of those memories brought a huge grin across her face as she thought about how she and Soleil started to get closer.

Flashback

The second she was finished with the listing of the items on the table, Soleil bounded over to them and threw his arm over the Hispanic woman's shoulders.

This action set her face ablaze and she tried not to squirm too much as she did not want to hurt his feelings.

"Hey, guys, Happy birthday little prince and princess! I got them both matching crowns! Also here are your party hats and here is one for you, Lia."

The nickname that came out of the Irishman's mouth sent her face on fire and the other three (3) eyebrows flew up into their hairline. Without a care in the world, he placed the crowns on the twins' heads and then the party hat on Ophelia's.

After doing this, he handed his friends' their own and smiled at them, then shooed them off for them to mingle with everyone else. That left him and the young chef alone by the drink table, which he did not mind in the slightest.

"You did a really great job today, Lia. I'm proud of you."

"T-thank you, Soleil."

"Anytime, doll."

End Flashback

By the time the Hispanic woman broke out of her inner musings, her haircut was finished and she was being ushered over to where Lyra stood near the wall of hair products.

Her eyes fluttered shut at the relaxing feeling of her hair being played with as they were detangled.

"Alright, honey, do you have any particular hairstyle you would like?"

"Umm, no. Do you have any idea though? I'm not very good with stuff like this."

"I think your face shape and the length of your curls, I'd go with a relaxed fishtail braid."

Ophelia hummed and nodded for her to go ahead with that particular idea. She liked the thought of it and on top of that, they did not have all the time in the world to contemplate.

It did not take a long time to finish up her hair, but the time was running out.

The brunette was swiftly moved over to where the clothing racks stood with several outfits that were meticulously planned out for her.

All of the outfits were absolutely stunning, but there was a certain piece that had caught her eye.

It consisted of a red-violet knit bustier top with bell-sleeves with a pair of black high waisted pleated trousers and matching ankle boots with block heels.

Something about it called out to her and she immediately pointed to it, declaring her choice.

Astrid had a smug look on her face that made the brunette realise that she was probably the one (1) who had put that outfit together.

Once she had gotten dressed and had finished admiring herself in the floor-length mirror that sat next to the station, she was whisked away again.

She was offered to have her makeup done for her, however, Ophelia politely declined as she actually enjoyed doing her own face. Picking up her moisturiser, she started from there and applied her products in the order she always did.

Ten (10) minutes later, she was finished getting ready and the clock said it was seven-thirty (7:30 PM). Her eyeshadow was neutral tones with a champagne glitter patted on the centre, with winged eyeliner and mascara.

She painted her lips with a wine red lipstick that she knew that her date liked on her. The only accessories she had on was the necklace he had gotten her a few weeks ago, along with a pair of diamond studs.

Everyone in the salon took a look at her and either clapped or let out loud whistles, letting her know that she looked beautiful. This caused a bright pink flush to spread across her cheeks and thanked them.

As she made her way over to the front door to leave the building to let her brother's boyfriend escort her to where her date was taking place, Zia stopped her.

"What's wrong?"

"You forgot your perfume."

"Oh, thank you."

She allowed herself to be spritzed with the Gucci Bloom, which smelled of spicy florals such as Chinese honeysuckle, tuberose and jasmine. It was one (1) of her favourite scents that her brother had gotten her.

Now she was fully finished getting ready and allowed to go on her way. Reid opened the door for her and offered his arm out to her in a gentlemanly manner. This action caused her to giggle as she looped her arm into his.

"Are you ready to go, m'lady?"

"I am, my dear sir."

"Well, onward to the venue we go!"

"You're an idiot."

"But you and your brother love me."

"True!"

24

"Are you ready to go, m'lady?"

"I am, my dear sir."

"Well, onward to the venue we go!"

"You're an idiot."

"But you and your brother love me."

"True!"

While Ophelia was getting ready.

Soleil and Reid were bustling around the giant garden that was located behind the castle trying to set up everything for the date later. After about fifteen (15) minutes had passed, he was called inside to cook their dinner.

Ivan, Elias, Benjamin, Nova and Kodiak switched places with him to help speed up the process of everything.

They had moments where one (1) of them had to stand on the shoulders of the other to reach a particularly high spot and they were too lazy to grab a ladder.

It certainly was a fun task to do and none of them complained as the heat of the dying sun caused them all toe perspire. The group was happy to assist in making sure that the new lovebirds' date night went flawless.

Once the garden was finished and everything was in place, they all went inside to see how the dinner preparations were being handled.

They knew that Reece was in charge of making the dessert and that was a godsend for the blonde man as he could not bake for the life of him.

Everything was going according to plan and before any of them knew it, the blonde had only a few minutes to get ready, which he managed to get done.

He was dressed in a pair of black dress slacks, an Olympic blue button-up and his signature combat boots.

He could not bring himself to have to wear oxfords or some other kind of formal footwear again as to him it was extremely uncomfortable.

He had on all of his silver rings, his thin Cuban link chain rested around his neck and all of his piercings had been cleaned to filth.

Now all Soleil had to do was go into the garden to wait by the dinner table while Reid came and escorted his lovely date to their decorated venue.

Present Time

Now it was time for his date to arrive and all he could think about was how he hoped she liked it and how hard his heart was hammering against his chest.

He heard the pair before they rounded the corner and once they did, he felt as if he was staring at an angel.

All he could think about was how she took his breath away every time he saw her. The young man was so gone for her and it showed all over his face.

The same could be said for the Hispanic woman because she was definitely in the same boat.

Ophelia finally turned her attention away from Reid and took in her surroundings, letting out a loud gasp at the beauty of it.

The stars were already out, along with the full moon, illuminating the night sky and creating the most breathtaking view.

Casting her gaze over to the trees, she saw that they had cool white glittering fairy lights strung up from the branches.

There were pastel blue, orange and purple lanterns hanging from the lower branches to cast a little bit more light onto the garden below.

The large outdoor pool had fake lilypads with or without flowers on top of them, floating on the water and the lights were changed to a lavender glow.

Turning to where her date stood by the seating area, her breath hitched. The decor was stunning.

An emerald green table cloth was draped over the round table with two (2) ivory with silver accents placemats. There was a swan origami folded napkin, with plum blossoms sticking out of it, seated on top of their empty plates and it was all amazing.

However, what really had caught her attention was the centrepiece. It was a large glass sphere that seemed to be filled with water and contained a pair of koi fish swimming inside.

It was lit up with underwater lights and connected to a pair of trees so that it was hanging a few feet over the middle.

She had no idea how they had managed to make that or how they even thought of the idea, but she loved it none the less. Reid discreetly nudged her forward and when she glanced back to glare at him, he shot her a cheeky wink before walking away.

Pale grey met chocolate brown and it was as if time had stopped. The outside world seemed to disappear and it felt as if it was just the two (2) of them alone.

Soleil moved first (1st), making his way over to the brunette and gently caressed her cheek with his index finger.

He watched as her eyes fluttered closed and she leaned into his touch with a look of absolute contentment on her face. Slowly, he leaned forward and their lips met.

The Irishman ran his tongue across her plump bottom lip, asking for entrance, which she quickly granted.

As soon as their tongues met, she released a quiet moan, which quickly turned into a louder one when she felt the silver ball that sat on top of his piercing.

The need for air soon became too great for either to ignore and unfortunately, they had to part.

"Babydoll, every moment with you is like a dream I would never want to fucking wake up from."

Soleil watched with immense satisfaction as her olive skin blushed bright red and her hands flew up to cover her face.

Chuckling, he gently pried her hands off and gave her a small peck on her head.

"Don't ever hide from me. You are the most captivating being I have ever been blessed to see."

"If you want me to stop hiding, s-stop saying words that make me all g-gooey."

"Gooey? Oh fuck, you are too adorable for this world, Lia."

"Oh hush! Anyways, before I die from overheating, I wanna say that this looks incredible, thank you for putting in all this effort. Words can't explain how much this means to me and I am not just talking about tonight, but for these past few months."

"You don't have to thank me for anything. You didn't deserve anything to happen to you and it still pisses me off to this day that I couldn't do anything sooner. I'm just glad that you are fucking alright now and are so strong. Now let's not sully our date with talk about the past, that could come another day, okay?"

"I agree wholeheartedly, b-babe."

"Cute, c'mon, let's go eat."

Taking her much smaller hand in his large one, Soleil guided her over to the eating area and like the gentleman that he was, pulled out her chair for her. The Hispanic woman shot him a grateful smile before carefully sitting down.

He proceeded to join her on the other side and smiled before he pressed a button that she had failed to notice was sitting on the edge of the wooden surface.

The backdoors of the castle opened and out came Reece, who was carrying two (2) dishes covered with silver domes.

Ophelia greeted her brother and watched wide-eyed as he placed their food in front of them. She released an audible gasp as he lifted it to reveal the delicious meal that was lying underneath.

The tantalizing aromas graced her nose and she could not help but let her eyes close as she breathed it in. Everything smelled divine and it was causing her mouth to pool with saliva.

It made it even better than it was her all-time favourite seafood dish.

"Tonight, Mr Walsh has been served pan-fried Maine lobster and scallops with asiago cheese tossed gnocchi. Miss Diaz-Walsh's dish is roasted asparagus with basil ricotta-stuffed salmon rolls with lemon sauce. Both dishes were made by your date, Mademoiselle. Bon Appétit!"

With a ridiculously overdramatic bow, the couple watched as their friend backed away still leaning down. It was a sight to see if they were being completely honest, they were surprised he did not trip and fall at any point.

Shortly after, Reid came through the opened doors with a large glass pitcher that was filled with a bright orange liquid and ice cubes were bobbing around inside.

Once he stood in front of them, he carefully poured them each a glass and offered them a small smile.

"Your date took into consideration that you are not a massive fan of alcoholic beverages and therefore tonight I am serving you, freshly made mango juice. This was made by Mr Walsh, please enjoy."

With that having been done, the pair were left alone with only the stars and the moon in the night sky to keep them company. Soleil raised his wine glass filled with the fruit drink and watched as his date did the same.

"To us and our future. May it shine as brightly as the stars, Lia."

"To us and our future. May our love be as big as the moon, Sol."

Their glasses clinked together as they cheered, soon after the pair started to eat their dinners and shared small talk.

Everything was perfect in Ophelia's eyes, she could not believe that this was her life now and she also could not be happier.

Her salmon rolls were perfection and when paired with the tangy lemon sauce, it was even better. The dressing left her lips tingling in a good way and the ricotta was smooth. The asparagus was roasted to the point where it was crispy, yet soft and chewy still.

As time passed they got to know one another on a deeper level as boundaries they were afraid to cross, were now being broken by questions. It felt so surreal for the two (2) of them, yet so right at the same time.

The entire night, since the moment the blonde's grey orbs met the sight of her, his heart was palpitating inside of his chest and his mind was just scrambled.

Although it may not have looked like it, he was fucking nervous and hard as hell.

Don't get him wrong, Ophelia's body in that outfit, accentuated her curves even more than ever, however, what was really getting him going was the way she looked at him.

Nothing else mattered to him.

The castle could be going up in an inferno and he would not give a shit as long as her eyes were on him. Those chocolate brown orbs swirled with so much passion and an unknown emotion that had him excited, that was enough.

Soleil averted his gaze from her before she could notice him staring at her with hearts practically shooting out of his eyes.

There was something that he wanted to do, however, it would have to wait until after they had their dessert and the date was coming to an end.

Not long after both of their ceramic plates were cleared and the button was pressed again. Once more the older men came out from the clubhouse and took the dishes, also refilling their glasses with some more juice.

Kodiak was the one (1) to deliver their sweet confections that had been chilling in the refrigerator for the past hour and a half.

The lovebirds greeted the young boy with warm smiles as he shakily placed their bowls down in front of them.

Ophelia opened her mouth to thank him when she realised that his hair was no longer a dark purple but now was strawberry pink. She couldn't help herself, so she raised her hand and ran it through his soft fluffy locks.

"I-Is everything alright?"

"Of course, I just noticed that you dyed your hair again."

"O-Oh, do you like it, Aunty?"

The Hispanic woman could feel her heart melt at the timid yet expectant look that washed over his face and the fact he had called, 'Aunty.'

"Yes I do, you look very handsome. The colour suits you very well, My little bear."

After chatting for a few more minutes, Kodiak informed them that the final course was made by his Dad. It was a coconut-strawberry ice cream pie with fresh strawberries garnishing the top and was made with homemade frozen yoghurt.

Soleil watched as the young boy walked away and he felt his soul come alive as pinkie looked back to give him an exuberant wave.

He was glad to see that he was no longer flinching at the smallest of things and was acting like a child his age.

He was broken out of his train of thought by Ophelia calling out his name, who telling him to hurry up and eat his frozen treat before it became soup instead.

Grabbing his spoon, he scooped out a large chunk and the second it met his tastebuds, he let out a loud groan.

Watching her love interest's eyes roll into the back of his head and hear him let out more sexual sounds over the pie made the brunette clench her thighs together.

She knew it was just his regular reaction to when something was delicious, but she couldn't help her body's reaction to it.

The fact that the blonde's voice was practically sinful did not help when he was making those noises. As if he was able to read her dirty thoughts, his eyes met hers and she watched as the corner of his lips curled up forming into a smirk.

He kept eye contact with her as he took another bite and did the same thing right after. In the back of his mind, he knew what he was doing to her, but willed his face to look fakely innocent and enjoy watching her squirm.

Soon though, their bowls were empty and their stomachs full. The Hispanic woman knew that this was basically the ending of their date and she really had no idea what was to happen from now going forward.

She opened her mouth to ask but was cut off by Soleil pushing back his seat and getting out of it to stand in front of her.

"Lia, from the day I met you, I knew you were going to be something so fucking special to me and now here we are. Our first (1st) date, can you believe it? I genuinely hope you had fun and enjoyed this as much as I have. However, that's not what this little speech is about. You are someone I want to protect, take care of, be able to make laugh, smile and hold. I have never felt as strongly as I do right now for someone. In the short period of time that we have known one another, I have fallen deeply for you and cannot see myself living without you. With that being said."

Ophelia watched with chocolate orbs blown wide as the Irishman got down on one (1) knee and pulled out of his pocket.

"A ring pop?"

"Yes."

"A ring pop."

"Moving on, would you do me the biggest pleasure in the world and be my girlfriend?"

"Of course, you dork."

"I love you, babydoll."

"I love you too, Sol."